THE PERFECT NEIGHBOR

LURING (Book #3)
TAKING (Book #4)
STALKING (Book #5)
KILLING (Book #6)

RILEY PAIGE MYSTERY SERIES
ONCE GONE (Book #1)
ONCE TAKEN (Book #2)
ONCE CRAVED (Book #3)
ONCE LURED (Book #4)
ONCE HUNTED (Book #5)
ONCE PINED (Book #6)
ONCE FORSAKEN (Book #7)
ONCE COLD (Book #8)
ONCE STALKED (Book #9)
ONCE LOST (Book #10)
ONCE BURIED (Book #11)
ONCE BOUND (Book #12)
ONCE TRAPPED (Book #13)
ONCE DORMANT (Book #14)
ONCE SHUNNED (Book #15)
ONCE MISSED (Book #16)
ONCE CHOSEN (Book #17)

MACKENZIE WHITE MYSTERY SERIES
BEFORE HE KILLS (Book #1)
BEFORE HE SEES (Book #2)
BEFORE HE COVETS (Book #3)
BEFORE HE TAKES (Book #4)
BEFORE HE NEEDS (Book #5)
BEFORE HE FEELS (Book #6)
BEFORE HE SINS (Book #7)
BEFORE HE HUNTS (Book #8)
BEFORE HE PREYS (Book #9)
BEFORE HE LONGS (Book #10)

THE PERFECT NEIGHBOR

(A Jessie Hunt Psychological Suspense Thriller-Book Nine)

BLAKE PIERCE

BLAKE PIERCE

Blake Pierce is the USA Today bestselling author of the RILEY PAGE mystery series, which includes seventeen books. Blake Pierce is also the author of the MACKENZIE WHITE mystery series, comprising fourteen books; of the AVERY BLACK mystery series, comprising six books; of the KERI LOCKE mystery series, comprising five books; of the MAKING OF RILEY PAIGE mystery series, comprising six books; of the KATE WISE mystery series, comprising seven books; of the CHLOE FINE psychological suspense mystery, comprising six books; of the JESSE HUNT psychological suspense thriller series, comprising eight books (and counting); of the AU PAIR psychological suspense thriller series, comprising three books; of the ZOE PRIME mystery series, comprising four books (and counting); of the new ADELE SHARP mystery series; and of the new EUROPEAN VOYAGE cozy mystery series.

ONCE GONE (a Riley Paige Mystery—Book #1), BEFORE HE KILLS (A Mackenzie White Mystery—Book 1), CAUSE TO KILL (An Avery Black Mystery—Book 1), A TRACE OF DEATH (A Keri Locke Mystery—Book 1), WATCHING (The Making of Riley Paige—Book 1), NEXT DOOR (A Chloe Fine Psychological Suspense Mystery—Book 1), THE PERFECT WIFE (A Jessie Hunt Psychological Suspense Thriller—Book One), and IF SHE KNEW (A Kate Wise Mystery—Book 1) are each available as a free download on Amazon!

An avid reader and lifelong fan of the mystery and thriller genres, Blake loves to hear from you, so please feel free to visit www.blakepierce-author.com to learn more and stay in touch.

TABLE OF CONTENTS

CHAPTER ONE

She didn't want to be nosy.

At least that's what Priscilla Barton told herself as she walked along the Manhattan Beach Strand with a bottle of Sauvignon Blanc in her hand.

Technically, Prissy, as she preferred to be called, was welcoming a new neighbor to the community. She and her husband, Garth, had been away at their Palm Springs estate for much of last week and must have missed the new people moving in. Since the Bartons returned to town, Prissy sometimes noticed the movement of a silhouette behind the always-drawn shades in the mansion next door. But she'd never seen anyone come in or out.

It was difficult to keep track these days anyway. Since so many of her neighbors in this wealthy, beach-adjacent stretch of town spent large chunks of the summer traveling, it was hard to know who was on vacation, much less who had rented or lent out their home.

Prissy knew that the owners of the house next door were a Hollywood agent and his wife, who ran some kind of scholarship fund for underprivileged youth. But they weren't especially friendly and were gone for long stretches of the year. In fact, she'd overheard another neighbor say they'd be gone until August. Since she hadn't seen them in weeks, it made sense that the person she'd seen was a renter.

As Prissy approached the front door, she felt a tingle of anticipation. What if the agent had lent out his house to a client, maybe a famous celebrity? It wouldn't be unusual. Lots of famous people lived or vacationed here. She could often spot them because they wore baseball caps, sunglasses, and ratty clothes. It was like their uniform.

Plus, they rarely looked up. If she saw someone who looked border-line homeless hiding their face and refusing to make eye contact, there was a solid chance it was a celebrity. Of course, she'd learned the hard way that sometimes it *was* a homeless person. So she was more cautious about approaching them than when she'd first moved in.

It wasn't like Prissy was a stranger to wealth. For the last nine years, she'd been married to Garth Barton, who was an extremely successful executive with Sharp Kimsey, an international oil and gas company. Until last year, they'd lived in the historic Hancock Park neighborhood, not far from all those gleaming downtown Los Angeles skyscrapers.

But Prissy, who had grown up poor and sweaty in Catahoula, Louisiana, had grown tired of the sweltering summer heat of central L.A. and demanded they move to the beach, which was usually fifteen to twenty degrees cooler. But living at the beach didn't mean being embraced by the locals. Prissy had yet to be accepted.

She liked to tell herself that it was because these were insular, aloof types who despised newcomers. And there was some truth to that. But deep down, she knew that it had a lot more to do with her sometimes grasping, social-climbing personality, the one she tried to hide but which always seemed to emerge at the most inopportune times.

She just couldn't help it. That aggressive persona had helped her scrape and claw her way out of the bayou to get to LSU, where she met the suave New Orleans boy who wanted to become a master of the universe.

After graduation and the wedding, Garth got the gig at Sharp Kimsey and they settled in Metairie, not far from the company's New Orleans office. They were transferred to Houston after two years and then to L.A. after four more. They'd been here for three years and Prissy loved it.

She loved the glamour of the town. She loved the unrepentant gaucheness. She loved the too-skinny women carrying around their too-tiny dogs in too-small purses. She wanted to be a part of it, even if her attempts made her look a little desperate. That's why she was currently standing at her neighbor's front door with a bottle of wine and a wide grin plastered on her face—to be a part of the scene.

She glanced back at the Strand, a pedestrian-friendly cement path that often came within a casual newspaper toss of many homes in the towns of Manhattan Beach and Hermosa Beach. It was surprisingly unpopulated for this late afternoon hour, which meant no one was around to judge her curiosity.

Prissy gave herself a once-over in the thick, shimmering glass of the door. She thought she looked good. At thirty-one, she still had the bouncy body she knew she needed in order to keep Garth's eye from wandering. All the yoga, Pilates, and beach boot camp workouts had paid off, keeping her tight in all the right places. Her dyed-blonde hair was loose around her shoulders and though it was early evening, she used the warm weather as an excuse to wear a sports bra and high-waisted yoga pants. She was pretty sure she'd make a good impression, whether the new resident was a celeb or not.

Prissy rang the doorbell but heard nothing. It must be broken. She knocked on the door and waited. There was no answer. She tried again and still got no response. She was about to give up and was debating whether to leave the wine on the doormat. But she hadn't brought a card and there was no way she was going to just leave the stuff without the recipient knowing who'd provided the gift. So she tried one last time. If no one answered this time, she'd just come back later. She banged hard on the door with the soft side of her fist. To her surprise, it opened inward slightly.

"Hello?" she called out loudly but tentatively.

There was no answer. Baffled by the oddness of leaving a multimillion-dollar home unprotected, she pushed the door open a bit more.

"Hi, it's your neighbor!" she called out as she peeked in the foyer for a pen and paper, anything to let the resident know that she deserved credit for the wine. Just leaving the bottle inside the door as an anonymous gift defeated the whole purpose of coming by in the first place. Seeing nothing, she closed the door behind her and stepped further inside the house.

"Hello! Anyone home? I swear I'm not here to rob the place. I have a housewarming gift. I'm just going to leave it in the kitchen."

She wandered down the cavernous hallway in the direction she assumed would lead to the kitchen. She felt slightly nervous. After all, she was trespassing. If someone was home and hadn't responded because they were in the shower or had earbuds in, they would be justified in reacting badly to an interloper sauntering into their home. But she also got a delicious thrill out of sneaking around.

She didn't meet a soul on the way to the kitchen. Every light in the house was off, which gave her the impression that the resident was gone and had just forgotten to lock or even properly close the door. She placed the wine on the kitchen island, found a pen, and wrote a short note on a nearby Post-it, which she stuck to the front of the bottle.

Slightly disappointed, she started back down the main hall when curiosity got the better of her again. As she reached the entrance to the large living room, she couldn't help but step inside and marvel at the place, which looked like it had been picked up and transported here directly from Cape Cod.

She was just considering pulling out her phone to snap a few photos so she could steal some ideas when she heard a rustling sound in the corner of the room. Looking over, she saw that it came from behind a large plant. For a second, Prissy thought she'd frightened a pet that was staying out of sight for safety.

But then, in a sudden burst of movement, a man shot out from behind the plant and ran toward her with a look of dark intensity on his face. Prissy felt an unexpected rush of panicked terror consume her. She wanted to scream but her throat had gone completely dry. The man was barreling right for her. She finally snapped out of it when she heard his breathing, heavy and fast.

She sprinted down the long hallway toward the front door. But running in beach sandals was awkward and after only a few steps, she lost her balance and tumbled to the floor. She scrambled to her feet again, minus one flip-flop. The sound of lumbering footsteps behind her made her whole body fire with adrenaline.

She was just reaching out for the doorknob when she felt a hard shove slam her forward into the door. Between that and her momentum, she smashed roughly into it and slumped to the floor again, gasping for breath. Before she could get back up, she felt something wrap around her neck.

She tried to slide her fingers underneath it. But she couldn't get any leverage and the man was twisting it tight as he yanked her back down the hall away from the door. She collapsed on top of him, sending them both to the floor hard. But he didn't let go.

Between the surge of adrenaline, getting the wind knocked out of her, and now being choked, Prissy felt her entire body screaming even if she couldn't do it out loud. She swung her elbows down, trying to hit her attacker in the ribs long enough to make him loosen his grip. But she could feel herself starting to lose consciousness and knew that her blows weren't having much impact.

It can't end like this!

The thought popped into her head as spotted lights began to consume her vision. The idea scared her enough to force one last, desperate attempt to shake herself free. But by then, it was far too late.

CHAPTER TWO

Jessie Hunt stood up from the kitchen table without visibly wincing.

She collected everyone's plates and walked over to the sink to rinse them off. As the worst cook in the group, she had escaped dinner prep duty. But that meant she was the official dishwasher. Normally it was a fair tradeoff. But since suffering her latest wounds, bending over the sink was a challenge. Putting dishes in the dishwasher was often cause for silent tears.

She still felt the sting where the skin on her back had been burned three weeks earlier. But she managed not to let it show. Neither her boyfriend, Ryan, nor her half-sister, Hannah, seemed to notice that she was still in considerable pain.

She'd suffered the burns while rescuing a woman from a disturbed man who'd abducted her and intentionally released her days later only to come back to her home intent on killing her. Jessie and the woman had barely managed to escape the burning house. Since then Jessie had been on leave from the LAPD, first stuck at the hospital and now in her own condo.

She knew it didn't have to be that way. She had lots of pain medication. The doctor had instructed her not to lower the dosage for a month. But she'd started weaning herself off it a week ago, partly worried about becoming dependent. But there was another reason too. She needed to stay alert.

On the day after Jessie was burned, while she was recovering in the hospital, her ex-husband, Kyle Voss, was released from prison. This was the same ex-husband who'd been incarcerated in the first place for murdering his mistress, trying to frame Jessie for the crime, and then attempting to kill her when she found out.

And yet somehow, the prosecutor in Kyle's case had recently confessed to improper conduct involving the mishandling of evidence. Of course Jessie knew the "somehow." Kyle had made friends with a prison gang associated with the infamous Monzon drug cartel. Subsequently, cartel members had threatened the prosecutor's family. Jessie was sure of this. Her FBI agent friend, Jack Dolan, was equally certain. Unfortunately they couldn't prove it.

So, while Jessie lay in a hospital bed recovering from burns, a judge released Kyle Voss into the community, even apologizing to him in court. Kyle was his usual charming self at the time. He held a press conference admitting he was "far from a perfect person" and that he planned to turn over a new leaf, including starting a foundation to fund charities that helped wrongly convicted prisoners.

What Kyle *didn't* admit to—what Jessie knew but couldn't prove— was that while he was in prison, he'd undertaken a campaign to destroy Jessie's life and reputation. It had started with small things, like having a cartel member knife her car tires. It escalated to planting anti-psychotic drugs, anonymously calling social services to claim she was abusing Hannah, whom she had custody of, and hacking into her social media and posting racist and anti-Semitic rants. That last maneuver, despite being unmasked, was still having lasting impacts on Jessie's work relationships and the public's perception of her.

It culminated with an anonymous flower arrangement sent to her hospital room saying the giver would be seeing her soon. Considering that Kyle had already tried to kill her and had told a prison informant that he wanted to "gut her like a pig and bathe in her warm blood," Jessie decided a little less pain medication was worth the discomfort if it kept her vigilant.

It helped that her boyfriend, who'd recently moved in with her and Hannah, was a decorated LAPD detective who looked like he could take a charging bull in a wrestling match. Ryan Hernandez, the top investigator in the department's Homicide Special Section (HSS) unit, was six feet tall and two hundred pounds of solid muscle. Jessie sometimes felt like she was dating her personal bodyguard, though it didn't look that way right now.

"Comfortable?" she asked as he moved over to the couch and lay down on it with his bare feet on the arm.

"Very," he said before teasing her. "You getting those dishes sudsy enough?"

"You're about to find out how sudsy they are if you don't take your smelly feet off the arm of my couch."

He complied without a word, though he did stick his tongue out at her. She tried not to grin.

In addition to having the tough guy in the food coma around, it was also reassuring that her apartment was essentially a vault. It had been designed that way when she was being hunted by her own birth father, a serial killer named Xander Thurman, who had decided that she would either join the family business or be a victim of it.

So she'd gotten a place in a building with retired cops as security guards, a 24/7 monitored, gated parking lot, and security cameras in every hallway and public space. But that was just the beginning.

She was one of the few residents—all in high-profile jobs—who lived on the secret thirteenth floor, which was unknown to most people in the building. It could only be accessed via stairwells from the twelfth or fourteenth floors, hidden behind utility closets.

In addition to all that, Jessie had set up her own elaborate security system for the condo, including multiple locks and alarms. The one advantage of having been married to a murderous but wealthy and successful financial advisor was that when she divorced him, she became independently wealthy herself.

Despite all those precautions, she knew that Kyle, a sociopath who had fooled her for a decade, was wily and relentless. He had almost gotten away with murder. He had negotiated his way out of a long prison sentence. She wasn't going to underestimate his ability to circumvent her security precautions.

"You up for dessert?" Hannah asked her from the dinner table, pulling Jessie back into the present as she rinsed off the last of the dishes. "I made pear tarts."

Jessie was full but didn't want to upset the tenuous good vibes of the evening.

"I'm about to burst but I could try a small one," she said, getting a satisfied smile from her half-sister.

Any smile she could get was a win these days. Though everything in the apartment seemed pleasant on the surface there was definitely some tension simmering just below. Ryan had asked for Hannah's permission first before broaching the idea of living together with Jessie. While the request was thoughtful, Jessie sensed that Hannah had consented more out of politeness than any genuine excitement.

It was clear that Hannah wanted her to be happy. But she also obviously didn't love sharing a two-bedroom apartment with an affectionate couple, especially when both of them were law enforcement professionals.

As Jessie considered this, Hannah walked over, pulled the tarts out of the oven and, without a word, dropped the tiniest one, which was also a bit charred, on the wet counter next to Jessie.

"Enjoy," she muttered.

"Thanks," Jessie said, choosing to focus on the offer of dessert rather than the manner in which it was delivered.

Sometimes Hannah's mild resentment came out in the form of passive-aggressive teenage jabs or, in this case, burned pear tarts. Sometimes it manifested through sullen silence. It wasn't constant but it emerged often enough to be noticeable. Her green eyes would turn stormy, her tall frame would get slouchy, and her sandy blonde hair would suddenly be tied back in a severe, disdainful ponytail.

The circumstances weren't ideal for Jessie and Ryan either, neither of whom felt they could really let loose romantically with a seventeen-year-old in a bedroom just across the living room. They'd been living together in this configuration for less than a month, but it was already becoming clear that a conversation about their future living situation was inevitable.

"With all the security you have here, maybe we could invest in some bedroom soundproofing," was the only quip Ryan had made on the matter.

And then there was the other thing, the one that hung over everything. Was Hannah Dorsey stable? Jessie had recently assumed custody of the half-sister she previously didn't know existed, having discovered her only after their shared serial killer father murdered Hannah's adoptive parents, and then another killer named Bolton Crutchfield had slaughtered her foster parents, kidnapped Hannah, and tried to indoctrinate her into becoming like him. It was a lot for anyone to recover from, much less someone in her junior year of high school.

"Please be careful with that knife," she said as Hannah carelessly used it to scrape the remaining tarts off the parchment paper on the tray.

"Thanks, Mom," Hannah muttered under her breath as she continued to use the blade like a scrub brush.

Jessie sighed without responding. The sight of her half-sister holding a long, serrated knife was disconcerting. Even as she tried to create a safe environment, she worried that perhaps some homicidal residue had been implanted in the girl. Had she secretly developed a blood lust after seeing the cruel power that violence offered those who embraced it? Was there some germ of murderousness that had somehow been passed down to her from her father? And if so, did Jessie have it too?

It was a question she'd brooded over for months. She addressed it with her therapist, Dr. Janice Lemmon, who had also been seeing Hannah. It was something she'd even asked her mentor, famed criminal profiler Garland Moses, to investigate. But no one could offer her anything definitive about Hannah's nature, just as she couldn't seem to discern a firm answer about her own character.

Most of the time Hannah just seemed like a regular teenage girl, with all the expected moods and hormones. But considering the trauma she'd suffered in recent months, sometimes even being "regular" seemed suspicious.

Jessie shook her head, trying to rattle the thoughts out of her brain. Right now, things were decent. Her sister had made dessert, even if she gave her the burned one. Everyone was being nice. Jessie was supposed to return to desk work next week and hopefully to full duty as a criminal profiler the week after that. Things were progressing.

Yes, it was frustrating to watch Ryan leave each morning, headed out to LAPD's Central Station, where they both worked. But she'd be joining him soon. Then she could return to the world she loved, where she got to catch killers by delving into their minds.

For half a second, the troubling nature of "loving" that world jumped out at her. But she swallowed the concern quickly, along with a bite of Hannah's excellent pear tart. Even slightly singed, it was delicious. As they were all finishing dessert, Ryan's cell phone rang. Even before he looked at it, everyone knew what it was about. At this hour, it was almost certainly a case.

"Hello?" Ryan answered.

He listened quietly for almost a minute. Jessie could barely make out the voice on the other end of the line. But based on the raspy, unhurried style, she was sure she knew who it was.

"Garland?' she asked when Ryan hung up.

"Yep," he said, nodding as he stood up and began gathering his things. "He's handling a case in Manhattan Beach and thinks it's a fit for HSS. He wants my help."

"Manhattan Beach?" Jessie pressed. "That's a little out of our jurisdiction, isn't it?"

"Apparently the victim's husband is a big-time downtown oil executive. He's heard of Garland and specifically requested him. He's supposedly a major asshole so the local cops are happy to play second fiddle to LAPD on this one."

"Sounds like fun," Jessie said.

"That's the weird thing," Ryan said, addressing not her but Hannah as he threw on his sports jacket and gun belt. "Most people would say that sarcastically. But your sister genuinely means it. She's jealous that she can't come along. It's a sickness."

He was right, in more ways than one.

CHAPTER THREE

Garland Moses felt guilty.

He'd been driving fast, trying to get to the crime scene as quickly as possible. As he drove west along Manhattan Beach Boulevard toward the ocean, he crested the top of the hill just as the last remnants of the setting sun cast a pinkish-orange glow over the beach town and beyond it, the Pacific Ocean.

Something about the sight loosened the tight ball of anticipation in his chest. Most people knew him as the crusty veteran profiler who rarely showed any emotion, much less something like awe. But alone in his car, he was free to gawk at the sight of surfers silhouetted against the crimson sun, with sailboats as their background. But even as he marveled at the postcard scene, the guilt started to creep in, telling him he wasn't here to appreciate the view. He was here on business.

Still, as he drove down the last stretch of road before it dead-ended at the pier, he glanced jealously at the crowds of people wandering the streets in summer attire. Though it was approaching 8 p.m., he still wore his unofficial uniform, a worn-out gray sport coat and a dull, off-white dress shirt. Normally he also added a sweater vest, but on this hot day that was too much even for him. He did, however, wear his traditional, faded navy slacks and badly scuffed brown loafers. The whole get-up was like a costume, designed to make suspects and witnesses let down their guard around the elderly, seemingly absentminded gentleman asking them personal questions.

He turned right on Ocean Drive, just a block from the beach. It was more of an alley than a street and he had to weave in and out of sloppily parked cars to get to the address he'd been given. When he arrived, he parked in a loading zone, put his LAPD placard on the dashboard, and got out.

He was immediately overcome by the combination of the cooling breeze and salty scent in the air, quite a change from his usual downtown haunts, which smelled more of exhaust and asphalt. He walked briskly until he arrived at the walking path that locals called the Strand. A half block north, he saw police tape and multiple officers blocking off part of the Strand to pedestrians.

As he headed in that direction, his investigative senses nudged his appreciation of his surroundings to the side. He still took in the sight of post-work volleyball matches on the sand and moms pushing strollers as they got in an evening jog. But he also studied the homes close to the crime scene.

They all faced the beach with doors that were only feet away from passersby. Very few had yards and almost none had protective gates. It seemed that in this neighborhood, ease of beach access trumped security precautions.

He felt slightly out of his element in this environment. Though he lived in central Los Angeles, he was embarrassed to admit that he rarely got to the beach, spending most of his time in the area surrounding the downtown station where he worked.

In that part of town, every homeowner or renter had some measure of security, whether it was a gate, bars on the windows, a security system, or all of the above. His friend and fellow profiler, Jessie Hunt, had all of the above, along with cameras, on-site security guards, a patrolled parking garage, and more door locks than light switches. Of course she had good reason. Still, he wasn't used to the laissez-faire attitude of this beach community. But he'd have to deal with it. He hadn't been given much of a choice.

Normally Garland Moses got his pick of cases. After all, for decades he'd been a celebrated FBI profiler in the Behavioral Sciences unit. Widowed young and childless, he'd been relentless about his work. When he finally moved to Southern California to retire, he'd been persuaded to work for the LAPD as a consultant. But only on the condition that he could choose the cases he wanted to pursue.

But not today. In this instance, Central Station's captain, Roy Decker, had pleaded with him to make an exception. The victim's husband, a wealthy oil and gas executive named Garth Barton, had given over $400,000 to the police union in the last three years. Though the couple now lived in Manhattan Beach, which had its own police department, Barton worked downtown and was well aware of the reputation of legendary profiler Garland Moses.

"Barton insists on bringing you in," Decker had told him over the phone. "He's hinting that his union contributions might end if you don't take the case. I'd consider it a personal favor, Garland."

Considering it was the first favor the captain had ever asked of him, he was inclined to do it. Once he said yes Decker continued talking quickly, as if worried Garland might change his mind.

"I promise that the MBPD will defer to you and your preferred team," the captain had assured him. "In fact, they seem enthusiastic about the prospect. Apparently Barton has a reputation as a real pain in the ass and they're more than happy to hand off dealing with him to someone else, especially when he's emotionally overwrought, as they say he seems to be now."

As Garland got closer to the cordoned off area of the Strand, he pushed the politics out of his head and returned his focus to the crime itself. He knew little, other than that Priscilla Barton had been found dead in a neighbor's house and that foul play was suspected. He arrived at the scene and looked around to see if Ryan Hernandez, the Homicide Special Section detective he'd asked to partner with him on the case, had arrived yet.

Not seeing him, he approached the closest MBPD officer and flashed his credentials.

"Garland Moses, LAPD forensic profiling consultant. Who's in charge here?"

The officer, whose name tag read Timms and who didn't look a day over twenty-two, gulped hard.

"Sergeant Breem is handling things until the detective gets here," he said, his voice quavering nervously. "He's inside right now."

"Mind if I join him?" Garland asked.

"No sir. He's in the foyer. That's where the body is."

"Thanks," Garland said. He started in that direction before stopping and turning around. "Did you know the Bartons, Officer Timms?"

"Not really," Timms said. "I never interacted with them personally but knew of them by reputation."

"How so?"

"Mr. Barton called in a lot with complaints about his neighbors, noise violations, stuff like that."

"And Mrs. Barton?" Garland pressed, scribbling notes furiously on his tiny pad.

"I don't want to speak ill of the dead," Timms said hesitantly.

"You're not speaking ill. You're just sharing information. And information is how we're going to catch her killer."

Timms nodded, seemingly convinced.

"Okay," he said, his voice dropping to a whisper. "She had a reputation as a bit of a celebrity stalker, harmless but annoying. A few times well-known folks who live here complained that she would follow them around, even try to buddy up to them, try to sit down and have drinks with them. It wasn't anything that serious. It's not like she was breaking into people's homes and waiting in bed for them."

"Are we sure about that?" Garland asked skeptically. "This isn't her house, correct?"

Timms's face turned red.

"I hadn't thought about it like that," he said, clearly embarrassed.

"Like what?" someone asked from behind them.

Garland turned around to find Detective Ryan Hernandez smiling at him.

"Never mind," he said. "How are you, Detective?"

"Considering I was ripped from the comforts of home and companionship, okay I guess. And yourself?"

"I'm actually quite enjoying the change of scenery," Garland confessed. "I almost don't want to go inside."

"And yet..." Ryan said reluctantly.

"...we must," Garland finished, waving his arm to indicate the detective should take the lead.

As Hernandez walked ahead of him toward the front door, Garland marveled at his younger counterpart. Even when he was in his early thirties, he never looked as put together as Ryan Hernandez. Of course, he didn't have the good looks of Hernandez either.

He had occasionally teased Jessie that her near-Amazonian height, deep green eyes, wavy brown hair, and well-defined cheekbones mixed with her boyfriend's short black hair, brown eyes, and well-defined pecs would ensure that their future children would eventually assume their rightful place on Mount Olympus. It almost always made her blush. He decided not to try the same crack with him.

They stepped inside where Sergeant Breem, a lanky, deeply tanned guy in his forties who Garland suspected was a surfer was waiting with two other uniformed officers and a crime scene unit. A deputy coroner was taking pictures of the body. The husband was nowhere to be found.

Garland looked around the foyer, making notes on his pad as he let his eyes take in everything. Only when he was sure he had a sense of the room did he look at the victim. Priscilla Barton was lying on her back with what looked like a stocking wrapped around her neck.

She had obvious burst blood vessels in her wide open eyes, a likely sign of strangulation. She was wearing a red sports bra, yoga pants, and one flip-flop. The other was lying forlornly halfway down the hall. There was no rigor mortis; she wasn't yet bloated and her skin was only slightly discolored, all suggesting her death was quite recent, likely not more than a couple of hours ago.

"Sergeant Breem," Hernandez said, extending his hand in introduction. "I'm Detective Ryan Hernandez with the LAPD. This is our profiler, Garland Moses. We appreciate you letting us participate in the investigation."

"Are you kidding?" Breem said, almost laughing. "We're glad to take a backseat on this one. Not to be insensitive, but Barton isn't an easy guy to root for. He's been nothing but a challenge since he and the missus moved here. We'll give you all the support you need but when it comes to dealing with that guy, we formally defer."

"Where is Mr. Barton?" Hernandez asked.

"He's at his house. It's right next door. If you listen closely, you can probably hear him yelling at my officer right now."

"We'll hold off on chatting with him for a bit then," Hernandez said, turning to the coroner, a youngish guy named Pugh. "What do you have so far?"

"Body temperature indicates she died less than three hours ago. Ligature marks and subconjunctival hemorrhaging strongly suggest strangulation. There's some bruising on the arms and chest, indicating a possible altercation before death. No sign of sexual assault so far."

"Anything else?" Hernandez asked.

Sergeant Breem piped in.

"We found a bottle of wine with a note in the kitchen. It looks like a housewarming gift from her. The note suggested the victim thought she had a new neighbor. But the couple that owns the house hasn't moved. They're on vacation but aren't renting the place out."

"That's odd," Hernandez said.

Breem nodded in agreement.

"We think someone may have been in the middle of robbing the place when she came over. Or possibly someone saw her go in and followed."

Hernandez looked over at Garland, who didn't comment on the theory. Instead he bent down near the body and studied the stocking still loosely wrapped around Barton's neck.

It was an odd choice for a murder weapon. Garland had seen lots of strangulations, many using wires, extension cords, and even bare hands. But he couldn't recall anyone ever being choked to death with a stocking.

It looks expensive.

He looked up, about to ask if anyone knew the brand. But seeing that the foyer was exclusively populated by men, he made a mental note to do some research of his own later.

"Can someone bag this?" he asked.

A crime scene tech stepped in to do exactly that, picking up the stocking with forceps and dropping it in an evidence bag.

"I doubt we'll be able to pull any prints off it," Breem muttered. "The place has been wiped clean of them. Whole sections of the house don't have any at all, not even from the homeowners. Whoever did this was diligent about cleaning up and seemed to wear gloves the entire time."

"Any chance of getting skin or hair fibers off the stocking?" Garland asked the tech.

"Possibly. But I see bits of material on it that also suggests the perpetrator might have been wearing gloves. We'll let you know."

Garland let Hernandez and the MBPD focus on the minutiae of the crime scene while he wandered around the house, trying to get a sense of what might have happened. There was no sign of an altercation anywhere else, which made him suspect that Breem's theory—that she was followed in or walked in on something—had merit. He knew she'd at least made it to the kitchen before anything happened. But where else she'd been in the home was a mystery.

"Garland!" he heard Hernandez call out.

He walked back into the foyer where everyone was looking at him expectantly.

"Yes?"

"Garth Barton wants to talk to you," Hernandez said. "He's insisting on it and supposedly getting snippy."

"Let's go," Garland sighed. "I wouldn't want to keep the VIP waiting. Where was he when this went down, by the way?"

"He volunteered that he was driving home and on a phone meeting the whole time," Breem told them. "He says his commute home takes about seventy to eighty minutes a day. We're confirming it all. But if he's being honest, he'll have an alibi for the window of death."

"That's unfortunate if true," Garland muttered under his breath.

"Why?" Breem asked.

"Because if it wasn't the husband, we've got a real challenge on our hands: highly trafficked area, little security to speak of, and minimal physical evidence." Then, unable to keep the weary cynicism out of his voice, he added, "I don't envy the people who have to solve this one."

CHAPTER FOUR

Kyle Voss woke up the next morning and bounded out of bed.
He dropped to the floor and immediately did a hundred push-ups. Then he did a three-minute plank, followed by fifty burpees. Happily drenched in sweat after only being awake for fifteen minutes, he went to the bathroom and stripped naked.

Staring at himself in the mirror, he couldn't help but admire his physique. Two years in prison may have put a pause on his professional life but it had done wonders for his body. He was harder and fitter than he'd been since his high school football days. At six foot two and an unyielding 215 pounds, he honestly thought he'd be passable as an NFL safety. His blond hair was still quite short, a remnant of his prison buzz cut. His blue eyes were clear.

He hopped in the shower, which he turned all the way to cold. He made sure to scrub every inch of his skin, refusing to hurry and refusing to shiver. When he was done, he toweled himself off and put on his favorite suit. This was an important day and he wanted to look good.

He'd been keeping a low profile since he got out of prison, laying the groundwork for his upcoming plans without drawing too much attention to himself. But all that would change today. This was the start of his public reinvention. It was crucial to his overall plan and had to go well. He felt a funny flicker in his stomach and eventually managed to identify it as nervousness.

The schedule for the day was quite involved. Even though the judge had dismissed his case, Kyle still had to meet with a parole officer twice a week. He didn't mind. Acing those sessions would pay dividends when his character was inevitably questioned down the line.

After that appointment, he had a meeting with his recently created foundation, WCP, which stood for the "Wrongly Convicted Project." It dispersed funds to charities that provided legal support to prisoners fighting false charges. It also allowed Kyle to perform some clever accounting magic, which he would eventually employ to help some friends he'd made behind bars.

After that, he had an interview with a local news station about the foundation. He'd been meeting with a media relations expert who'd taught him how to focus on the foundation without getting caught up in unpleasant conversations about the reason he was convicted in the first place—that whole mess with Jessie. This would be his first attempt to navigate those choppy waters.

Once the news interview was over, he had one of another kind. He was meeting with a wealth management firm based out of Rancho Cucamonga, not far from his Claremont townhouse. He'd moved to the charming college town, over thirty miles from downtown Los Angeles, so that no one could credibly accuse him of trying to intimidate his ex-wife. And if the interview went well (he'd been assured by his friends in Monterrey that it would) he'd have an imprimatur of legitimacy that would be crucial to the work he had planned in the coming weeks and months.

He needed the credibility that came with a position at a well-respected firm. And though he didn't like to admit it, he needed the money too. He'd made a pretty penny before the whole murder thing. But the divorce from Jessie and his legal defense had drained much of his resources. He still had access to funds he'd cleverly squirreled away during the marriage. But that wasn't enough to run the foundation, support the lifestyle he wanted, and finance the total destruction of his ex-wife's world. He simply needed more income.

He was just finishing up breakfast when the front doorbell rang. He checked the security camera using his phone and saw that it was his parole officer, which wasn't a total shock. He'd been warned that unscheduled home visits weren't uncommon and to be prepared.

"Hi, Mr. Salazar," he said, opening the door. "I thought we were supposed to meet up at your office at nine. Just couldn't wait, huh?"

"You're aware that unannounced home visits are permitted, Mr. Voss?" Salazar asked crisply.

"Of course," Kyle said as if he'd been expecting him. "I figured that after so many trips to your place that you'd return the favor at some point. I was just finishing up breakfast. Can I offer you anything? Coffee? I make a mean cheesy egg scramble."

"No thank you. This needn't take too long. I just wanted to see what you had planned for the week to make sure you were meeting your court-ordered obligations."

"Sure thing," Kyle said warmly, turning and heading back into the house. "My calendar is in the kitchen."

Salazar followed him cautiously. Kyle continued to act as if they were just old buddies catching up, pouring the man a cup of coffee and putting it on the table across from him. Salazar, despite his earlier protestations, took a sip.

Kyle walked the man through the very itinerary he'd been assessing only moments earlier, minus a few details, of course. He could tell within minutes that Salazar was satisfied but kept going, poring over every appointment he had all week. The goal was to be so forthcoming that Salazar didn't feel the need for another in-home visit any time soon.

It worked. Less than ten minutes later the parole officer was leaving, along with a to-go cup of coffee and a plastic container of cheesy eggs he'd changed his mind about.

"See you on Friday," he reminded Kyle. "Nine a.m. sharp in my office."

"Looking forward to it."

Five minutes later he was out the door himself. As he got into his car and waved at the FBI agents parked across the street, where they'd been intermittently since he moved in, he mentally reviewed his schedule. He knew that in between all the meetings and interviews, it would be challenging to organize the metaphorical and physical destruction of Jessie Hunt. But he was confident that he could do it. After all, he'd already stage-managed the near collapse of her career from behind bars.

With the formidable assistance of the Monterrey-based Monzon drug cartel, he'd coordinated all manner of nightmares for Jessie. It had started small, having the cartel soldiers knife her car tires. It escalated to planting drugs, making anonymous calls to social services suggesting she'd abused her sister, and best of all, hacking into her social media and posting racist rants. That one was still resonating, making his ex-wife persona non grata with many in L.A., even after she was technically exonerated.

The cartel was helping ensure that there would still be protests outside the station where she worked. Her car was scheduled to be tagged with graffiti soon. And then the good stuff would start.

First, there would be the elimination of those closest to her. And then, when she was at her most emotionally vulnerable, he'd come for her and do what he'd been dreaming of for years now. At first he'd planned to slice her open and watch her face fill with horror as he cut out her organs and burned them in front of her. But now he actually had something far worse in mind for her. Payback would be a bitch for this bitch.

CHAPTER FIVE

Jessie nibbled at her muffin nervously.

As she sat in the Nickel Diner on South Main Street, waiting for Garland Moses to arrive, she had the weird feeling that someone was cheating. Usually she and Ryan worked together. But Ryan had investigated a case with Garland last night in Manhattan Beach. Was their team-up a personal violation of some sort? Was this morning's breakfast get-together? She knew that logically, it was ridiculous. And yet the feeling lingered.

Garland finally shuffled in at 8:30 a.m., a full half hour after they were supposed to meet. His white hair seemed even wilder and more disheveled than usual. His bifocals appeared to be in danger of tumbling off the tip of his nose. He didn't even look up as he made his way to the booth Jessie knew he preferred.

She caught the server's eye and motioned for her to bring over some coffee for the guy, who looked wiped out. After being up so late, she would have been too and she was thirty, not seventy-one.

"Rough night?' she asked as he slid into the seat.

He smiled ruefully.

"I was up way past my bedtime," he admitted. "As I'm sure your boyfriend can attest to. I could really use some coff—"

He stopped speaking as a mug was placed on the table and filled up.

"You read my mind," he said to the server, who pointed at Jessie.

"Actually, *she* did."

"That's some quality profiling," he said as he took a careful sip.

"That's not profiling, Garland. Knowing you want coffee when you walk in here is like knowing the sun rises in the east."

"Thanks all the same," he said.

"How did it go last night?" she asked.

"Hernandez didn't tell you?"

"He was leaving when I got up. He didn't want to wake me, keeps telling me to rest and stuff."

"Maybe you should listen to him," Garland suggested protectively. "You *are* recovering from multiple burns, a concussion, and a bruised stubborn bone."

"Is that you trying to be funny, Garland?" she asked. "Because if it is, you should definitely stick with your day job, which is apparently also now a night job."

"Don't try to change the subject," Garland countered. "I know you're trying to get back to work earlier than the doctor wants and you shouldn't do it. Wait until your body is ready."

"How do you know I'm trying to get back early?" she demanded.

"Easy," he answered with a mischievous smile. "Any time you bend or twist, you involuntarily wince a little, which tells me you're taking a lower dose of your pains meds than was prescribed. Also, you keep leaning forward like a schoolgirl worried the nun will slap your hand for slouching at your desk."

"What does that have to do with anything?"

"You're afraid to let your back bump the back of the booth because it's still tender. So you've adopted the primmest posture I've seen outside an E.M. Forster novel."

She shook her head in both frustration and amazement.

"It's almost as if you should do this professionally."

"Flattery will you get everywhere," he said, taking another sip. "But I'm serious. You should take it easy as long as you can. Plus, staying out of the public eye might help the backlash from those racist posts subside a bit."

"The posts I didn't write?" Jessie reminded him.

"That's not the point anymore," he said resignedly. "No matter how much proof you offer that your account was hacked, some people are still going to want to assume the worst of you."

"So you think I should just lie low until people forget that they think I'm a racist?" Jessie said skeptically.

Garland sighed but refused to take the bait.

"Maybe do what your friend Kat is doing," he suggested.

Jessie's friend, private detective Katherine "Kat" Gentry, was currently getting a full neurological workup at the Mayo Clinic in Phoenix. She'd been with Jessie during the rescue of the abducted woman from the burning house. They'd both suffered concussions when a bomb exploded at the scene.

For Kat, who'd served as an army ranger in Afghanistan and prided herself on ignoring her scars, both external and internal, this was at least her sixth. She'd finally consented to get checked out when the headaches and ringing in hers ears hadn't subsided after two full weeks. She would be in Arizona for five days before returning this weekend.

"Kat's a military veteran dealing with PTSD, IED injuries, and possibly CTE," Jessie told him. "I'm just a gal who got a few burns."

Garland smiled paternally.

"That was quite the alphabet soup there, Jessie. And while it's true that your friend is dealing with potentially serious issues, so are you. You've been concussed multiple times. And you've got more scars, physical and emotional, than most soldiers. How many of them were tortured by their own birth father after watching him murder their mom?"

"Probably a few," Jessie snapped snarkily.

"And how many of them had to take on that same father in a fight to the death? And later kill his serial killer protégé? *And* tangle with her sociopathic killer of an ex-husband? And…"

"I get it, Garland," Jessie interrupted.

He sat quietly for a moment.

"I'm just saying you need to take care yourself. If you won't do it for your own well-being, think of your little sister and that dashing detective you love. Those relationships are inevitably going to suffer if you keep your foot on the pedal all the time. Looking out for you helps you look out for them."

She nodded, taking another small bite of the muffin she was no longer interested in.

"I noticed you changed the subject too," she pointed out.

"What?"

"The case? Did you solve it?"

"Any minute now," he said wryly.

"Are you going to actually tell me anything at all about this case?" she asked, annoyed.

"Dead woman found in a neighbor's home," he said matter-of-factly. "We eliminated the husband, which disappointed me because he's a genuinely unpleasant person. I would have loved to have nailed him for it. But at least that means I don't have to interact with him anymore. He was like a walking, talking ulcer."

"What else?" she asked.

He looked at her with an odd expression, as if he wanted to ask her something but couldn't think of how best to broach the subject.

"Do you consider yourself a fashion plate?" he finally asked.

Jessie hadn't expected that one.

"I can dress myself," she said. "But do I have a subscription to *Vogue*? No. Why?"

He started to speak, but then stopped himself, instead taking a sip of coffee.

"Is that it?" she demanded. "Aren't you going to expand on that?"

"I don't think so," he told her. "I've already said more than I should have. I worry that anything else I tell you will be like catnip and you'll just want more. You're supposed to be recuperating and I don't want to undermine that. If you really want the particulars, pump Hernandez for them."

"Ugh," Jessie said. "That was the only reason I asked you to meet me."

"And here I thought you just wanted the pleasure of my company. That's very hurtful." He sounded wounded but she could see a grin starting to form at the corners of his mouth.

"You are a very unpleasant man," she said. "You know that, don't you?"

He took another sip of coffee and allowed himself the full-on smile this time.

"Did you want to discuss any non–case related topics?" he asked. "I feel like you're holding back."

"What am I holding back?" she replied more petulantly than she'd intended.

"We haven't talked about Hannah in a while. How's she doing?"

Jessie exhaled deeply.

"Sometimes sweet. Sometimes moody. Sometimes hilarious. Sometimes bitchy. Sometimes silent. Your basic nightmare."

"But no killing, right?" Garland said.

"What?"

"The half-sister you're worried might be a budding, sociopathic serial-killer-in-training—she hasn't murdered anyone yet?"

"Not to the best of my knowledge," Jessie answered.

"Then moody doesn't seem so bad in comparison," he noted.

She shrugged in agreement.

"Not when you put it that way."

"Maybe count your blessings," he said mildly. "Considering the life you lead, things could be a hell of a lot worse."

Jessie couldn't deny that. She was about to ask him for his input on another matter when her phone rang. She looked down. It was her FBI agent friend Jack Dolan, who'd been having his people keep tabs on her ex-husband, Kyle.

"I have to take this," she said.

"That's okay," Garland, said, dropping a five on the table. "I should get into the office anyway. Your boyfriend probably misses me."

"You want a ride?"

"Nah. You've got your call. Besides, you know I like to walk."

"Okay," she said as she answered the phone. "Hi, Dolan."

"Hey, Jessie," Garland added in a hushed voice as he stood up.

"Hold on one second, Dolan," she said into the phone before looking up at the crusty guy in front of her. "Yeah, Garland?"

"Just remember, you're in charge of your life. Not Decker, not Hannah, not Hernandez, and not any serial killer. Sometimes it's hard to see it that way. But you always have choices."

"Thanks, Confucius," she said as she winked at him. "We'll talk later, okay. I've got to take this call. It's about Kyle."

Garland smiled, bowed slightly, and headed out, his shock of unruly white hair fading into the distance as he disappeared leisurely into the crowd of people hurrying to their destinations.

"I'm back," Jessie said. "What have you got for me, Jack?"

"Bad news—it's about your ex-husband."

CHAPTER SIX

"Hang on a minute," Jessie said, even as her heart dropped into her stomach. "I need to find somewhere private to talk."

Jessie almost regretted waiting. The three minutes it took to pay, leave the diner, and get into her car felt interminable. Dolan, a hard-bitten cynic whose attitude was only mildly tempered by his morning surf outings, was not known for hyperbole. If he said a situation was bad, it was usually worse. She thought she might throw up the quarter of a muffin she'd eaten.

"Tell me," she said brusquely when she took him off hold.

"The short version is: we've got nothing."

"It's been over three weeks," she protested. "You're telling me he's been a perfect citizen this whole time?"

"Yep," Dolan said, "suspiciously so. He hasn't so much as rolled through a stop sign. Of course, he's well aware that we're watching him. He waves at our agents when he drives by."

"They're not trying to stay low profile?"

"They were at first. But he's pretty savvy, as you know. He spotted our van the first week so it seemed like a waste to use it after that. We've been employing unmarked sedans ever since. The truth is that my bosses are balking at the use of resources as it is. Pretty soon, they're going to make me pull back to one agent. I wouldn't be surprised if they dump the surveillance entirely by the end of the week if nothing pops. By then, it'll have been a month without anything."

"But that's exactly what he's waiting for," Jessie insisted. "He's holding out until you pull your guys before he tries anything big."

Jessie could feel a familiar anxiety resurfacing, as she recalled how adept her ex-husband was at presenting a charming front that masked the ugliness below.

"You know that and I know that," Dolan said, clearly frustrated. "But that doesn't mean much to the higher-ups. They want to see results. And we haven't given them any. You have to look at it from their perspective."

"What does that mean?" Jessie demanded.

"Remember, technically your ex-husband was released because of malfeasance by a law enforcement professional. They don't want to be accused of harassing a man who was already mistreated by the system. It's a political issue. The fact that he's a murderer gets lost in there. So we've had to tread lightly as it is. We're close to the point where the hope of catching him in illegality is being outweighed by the bad press that might blow back on us. Today might be a tipping point on that front."

"Why?" Jessie asked, though she could already guess. Kyle was about to go into public relations mode.

"Because later this morning, he's scheduled to do an interview with a news station," Dolan said, confirming her intuition. "Technically, it's about his foundation. But I wouldn't be shocked if his current personal situation comes up. And my supervisor is worried he might mention the surveillance."

Jessie realized she was sweating, though she wasn't sure whether it was because of Dolan's words or the fast-rising morning temperature. She turned on the ignition and jacked up the air-conditioning.

"What about the suspicion that he's involved with the Monzon cartel?" she asked. "Aren't they worried that if they pull surveillance they'll miss it if he contacts them?"

"We have other potential ways of keeping tabs on him. We got judicial authorization to put a tracker on his car, to set up bugs and cameras in his house, even to monitor his calls. But considering that a judge just gave a prosecutor a tongue-lashing for overreach—"

"A prosecutor who was surely threatened by the cartel," she interrupted.

"Which we can't prove," Dolan countered. "My bosses are worried that the judge who authorized the taps will be wary about extending surveillance if he thinks his reputation is at stake. We're in a delicate situation here."

Jessie shook her head, though no one could see it. Less than a month and Kyle was already manipulating the system to his advantage. She bristled at the thought of what he could do with another month of freedom.

"This is exactly what he wanted, you know," Jessie pointed out. "He knows you're tailing him but he hasn't complained yet. He's holding it over your heads, ready to bust it out when he needs it most. He's keeping his nose clean as long as it serves his purposes. He doesn't want to cry to the press if he can get you guys to back off without it. He's saving that chit. This is all part of his setup."

She heard Dolan sigh heavily through the phone.

"You don't have to convince me, Jessie," he assured her. "I'm on your side. I'm just wondering if maybe we should pull our guys back now, before he makes any accusations. Then we can legitimately claim we're not following him, harassing him. I can craft the message for the press that we merely have agents check in on him from time to time. If it looks like he's Chicken Little, it hurts his credibility. He's not the only one who can play this game."

"No, but he's better at it than anyone I've ever met. Don't underestimate him."

"I won't," Dolan promised. "Listen, we know that Kyle is out of jail because he convinced the cartel it was worth their time and effort. We know they were even willing to help destroy your life for him. At some point, he's going to have to deliver for them. Something is going to break with this guy soon."

"Yeah, I just hope it breaks before he finds a way to break me."

Jessie could tell Ryan was trying not to rub it in.

"How were your days?" he asked her and Hannah as he washed the broccoli for dinner, pointedly making no mention of the case.

Hannah was prepping a marinade for the lamb while Jessie searched for the broiling pan.

It was clear that he hoped that by keeping quiet about his own day, he wouldn't make her jealous that he was out investigating murders while she was stuck in the apartment. She thought it was a sweet gesture, though he would soon learn it was futile.

"Only two more weeks of school," Hannah said happily. "Then it's summer break. So there's that."

"That's awesome," Ryan replied.

"Don't forget that you have summer school," Jessie reminded her, hating how schoolmarmy she sounded.

"I know," Hannah said, dialing up the sarcasm. "But that's at the 'regular kids' school and not the therapeutic high school for students 'facing extreme emotional and psychological challenges.' Besides, it's not for another month. Please don't crush my already fragile spirit."

"Sorry," Jessie said.

"And your day?" Ryan asked Jessie, quickly changing the subject.

"It could have been better," she admitted. "Dolan told me they can't nail Kyle for anything. He's been a choir boy since he got out. They're thinking of pulling surveillance."

"That sucks."

"It does," she agreed. "Almost as much as having my friend and professional mentor shut me down when I tried to get details on the case he was working because he was worried I'd salivate right in front of him."

"Uh-oh."

"Uh-oh what?" she asked.

"Uh-oh, Garland warned me you might come at me hard for info because he wouldn't share much."

"Oh yeah?" she pressed. "Did he give you any advice on how to handle me?"

"He said to stay strong, not to crumble under your withering interrogation."

Jessie smiled malevolently.

"How do you think that's going to go for you?"

31

"I'm confident that I'll hold up," he said, as he walked toward their bedroom. "But first I'm going to take a shower."

"You know that stalling tactics will only work for so long," she shouted as he disappeared from sight without responding.

Jessie stared at the door, wondering if she could perhaps burn it to ashes with her eyes alone.

"Ahem," Hannah muttered tentatively. "I hate to pile on when you're already so salty, but the lamb I was going to broil smells funny. I think we're going to have to toss it out, which means we have no dinner plan."

Jessie felt her shoulders sag involuntarily. This day was ending as badly as it had started.

"I've got it covered," she finally said.

"Please don't tell me you're going to try to cook something?" Hannah said, sounding genuinely concerned.

"You know, I managed to get dinner on the table almost every night for years before you started living here. Have a little faith."

"*Almost* every night?" Hannah repeated.

"Some nights I wasn't that hungry," Jessie said defensively.

"Right," Hannah said, unconvinced. "You're ordering pizza, aren't you?"

Jessie felt a twinge of shame as the words came out.

"Yes. I'm ordering pizza."

CHAPTER SEVEN

By the time Garland crested the hill, the sun had already set.
As he made the now-familiar drive down into Manhattan Beach, he could still see the ocean where the waves broke close to the beach. But it didn't have quite the same majesty as last night, when dusk was only starting to take hold.

He told himself that it didn't matter, that he had come back here for the second night in a row because of the investigation, not because of the view. But even he wasn't totally convinced. Yes, something about the crime scene was eating at him. But the truth was, he was also looking for an excuse to walk along the breezy surfside streets with their patio restaurants and wine store tastings.

He found a parking spot near the main drag and got out, wandering up Highland Avenue to the police station. Along the way, he could smell what he thought were short ribs wafting out of a café on the corner. He passed a newsstand with papers from New Zealand and India and fought the urge to stop and peruse them.

Instead he walked the final block to the station, giving the desk sergeant his name. Officer Timms from the prior night came out and gave him the key to the home of Charles and Gail Bloom, where Priscilla had died.

"I can go with you if you like," the young officer offered. "I'm on overnight duty and it's been pretty quiet."

"Thanks," Garland replied. "But sometimes I like to walk through the scene on my own, without any distractions. I find it helps me uncover things I might have missed before. But I promise to return the key within a few hours."

After he left the station, Garland strolled casually down the steep walking path to the Strand. At this hour, approaching 9 p.m., it was mostly quiet. There were a few runners and some people taking their dogs on the last walk of the night. In fact, he had to sidestep the urine trail of one particularly sloppy canine.

He ambled the last half block to the Bloom house, taking in the sound of crashing waves and gulls calling out to each other. He knew that once he walked in that house, his brain would go into overdrive and all the little pleasures he was currently appreciating would be immediately forgotten. He was just trying to delay the inevitable.

When he arrived, he slipped under the police tape, making sure to stay in the shadows so recent widower Garth Barton wouldn't see him if he happened to be looking out a window. Just because the man had been cleared didn't mean he wasn't a jerk. Garland was happy to let the locals handle that headache.

He unlocked the front door and stepped inside. The house was dark, though he could still see the chalk outline where Priscilla Barton's body had been found. Looking at the spot, he recalled the conversation Detective Hernandez had described having with the homeowners earlier in the day.

It amazed him that even learning a woman had died in their foyer wasn't enough to get them to return from their vacation. Unfortunately, with them and the husband eliminated as suspects, he was hitting a wall. That's why he was here: to find a fresh perspective.

He did a cursory walk through the first floor before going to the second, which was the reason he'd returned in the first place. Something had been bothering him all day but he hadn't put his finger on it until he was driving home. Once he realized what it was, he was almost home. Instead of continuing, he'd turned the car southward and headed back to the Blooms' mansion. Along the way, he called the MBPD to tell them he wanted to check out the scene again and was informed that a key to the house would be left for him.

At the top of the stairs, he turned on his small flashlight and made his way down the hall to the master bedroom. After allowing himself a moment to take in the large room with the canopy bed, he moved over to what he assumed was Gail Bloom's dresser. Though he felt like a bit of a pervert, he slid on his gloves and pulled open the top drawer, which he assumed held her undergarments. Sometimes the job called for unusual choices.

He shined the flashlight into the drawer as he delicately moved around the woman's delicates. After a thorough going-through, he pulled out his phone to once again look at the apparent murder weapon used on Priscilla Barton—the stocking. The brand, called Only the Best, which he'd learned after doing some online research, was very high end.

But looking through Gail Bloom's drawer, he had found no pairs of that brand or any other hose at all, for that matter. Nor did he find a solo stocking, either in the drawer or on top of it. He knelt down to see if it might have fallen under the dresser but found nothing.

He got out his notepad and briefly noted his conclusion—that Bloom didn't seem to own these stockings. That was odd and potentially helpful news. If the stocking wasn't hers, then the killer hadn't just grabbed it on the fly and used it as a makeshift weapon. He or she must have brought it into the house.

But why? Who walks around with a single, fancy piece of women's hosiery?

His thoughts were interrupted by the sound of a creak on the floorboard behind him. He slid his notepad back into his jacket pocket and stood up slowly, though his thoughts were racing wildly.

He could hear the sound of muffled, heavy breathing several feet away and actually sensed the body heat emanating from someone else in the room. He gripped the small flashlight hard, well aware that it was the only thing close to a weapon he had.

He tried to remember his training from his youthful FBI days but that was over forty years ago. The closest he'd gotten to a physical altercation recently was when a skateboarder accidentally knocked him over last year while zipping past him on the sidewalk.

In the end, Garland decided to simply let adrenaline and instinct do their work. But he wasn't going to wait for the attack to come to him. So, as quickly as his aching bones would allow, he spun around and flashed the light in the direction of the heavy breathing.

He immediately saw his assailant, who was wearing black clothes and a black ski mask and holding a leather belt in his hands. Though the face wasn't visible, the frame suggested a male. Garland took a step toward the man, who held his hand up to block the light and lurched forward. They collided hard but the other man's weight advantage sent Garland sprawling back into the dresser. His bifocals flew off. He felt the dresser's wood edges slam into his back and grunted.

He tried to ignore it and focus on the figure, who was still coming at him fast. As the man rushed forward, Garland swung his flashlight upward, making solid contact with the spot just below the attacker's left rib cage. The man inhaled sharply as he doubled over, allowing Garland to shove him to the ground.

He stepped around the man and dashed toward to the bedroom door. Even at this short distance away, it looked blurry without his glasses. About three steps from the hallway, he felt a hand grab hold of his right ankle and tug, making him lose his footing and fall to the floor. As he did, he heard a crack and a searing pain cut through his right hip. He cried out despite himself.

Garland tried to ignore the burning sensation. He wanted to roll over so he wouldn't be in such a vulnerable position but his body wasn't complying. Instead he did the only thing he could think of. He tried to crawl out of the room. The agony made his eyes water but he dragged himself along anyway. That's when he felt the weight of the other man climbing on top of his waist.

The physical distress was unbearable as waves of pain radiated out from his hip. But that was nothing compared to the clenching grip of fear he felt envelop his entire body. There was a man on top of him holding a belt and there was nothing he could physically do about it.

He had the briefest flash of recognition, aware that he was going through the same moment of terror that so many victims he'd seen had experienced. Then, deciding he would not join their ranks, he stopped struggling to escape and instead pressed his forehead into the carpet as he pulled his fists up to his neck to preemptively protect it.

A moment later, he felt the belt swing over his head, felt the man try to wrench it between his forehead and the carpet to get it around his neck.

The yanking motion tore some of the skin off his forehead as it ripped downward. Ignoring it, Garland opened his balled up fists and grabbed the belt so the backs of his palms created a barrier between the belt and his throat.

The man on top of him didn't seem to care. He pulled up hard so that Garland's own knuckles were squeezing into his Adam's apple, making him gasp for air. The smell of his own latex gloves filled his nostrils. He took a big gulp and tried to hold the belt off while he thought of something he could do.

He looked around desperately. Everything looked indistinct. Still, there had to be something nearby he could grab or some maneuver he could try. There had to be some way to outwit his attacker. Forty-five years of stopping killers couldn't end this way.

But there was nothing—nothing to grab, no way to shout. He was stuck. He was going to die on this carpet in this house, just yards from people waiting for their pets to do their business so they could settle in for the night. He was out of options.

But as his breathing became labored and his thoughts grew fuzzy, he realized that wasn't quite true. He might not live through this but at least he could provide a clue as to who did it. Detective Ryan Hernandez would surely investigate his death. And if he did, he would consult with Jessie Hunt. If Garland could provide any clue as to who had done this, Jessie might uncover it. If anyone could, it was her.

So he resolved to do the only thing he could think of. He pressed his body downward toward the carpet as forcefully as he could, pulling hard away from the man above him. Then, when he felt the man pulling his hardest, he stopped fighting and allowed himself to be yanked upward, throwing his head back aggressively.

He had been hoping to make contact with the man's face, to leave a visible bruise. Instead he felt the back of his skull slam into something hard but less prominent. He heard a crack. The man yelped and released his grip slightly. Garland guessed that it was the man's clavicle.

For a fraction of a second he was tempted to try to wriggle free, but knew that would be fruitless. The other man still had the advantage. Instead, he used the brief respite to take another gulp of air and slam his head back again. The scream from the man told him he'd once again hit the target.

But then the man seemed to find a new reserve of strength and fury. Garland felt the belt squeeze tighter than before and found that he could no longer make fists to grab it. He could actually feel the blood pumping through his carotid artery as it pressed against the back of his hand. Another violent tug crushed his trachea and he heard himself rasping softly.

All of a sudden, he noticed that the pain in his hip, back, hands, and throat was subsiding. He wondered what could be causing it. And then, with his last coherent thought, it occurred to him: he was losing consciousness for what would be the final time.

CHAPTER EIGHT

Jessie sat bolt upright in bed.

The sound of Ryan's ringing phone had ripped her from the best night of sleep she'd had in weeks. She recognized the ring tone immediately. It was Captain Decker. She glanced over at her bedside clock. It was 2:46 a.m. For the captain of their station to call at this hour, it had to be something serious.

"Hello," Ryan mumbled after fumbling with the phone for several seconds.

Jessie could hear Decker's voice but he was speaking more quietly than usual and she couldn't make out any words. She did notice Ryan's body visibly stiffen.

"Okay," he said quietly as he turned on the light and sat up in bed.

Decker continued talking for another half minute while Ryan listened, never interrupting.

"I will," he finally said, before hanging up.

"What is it?" Jessie asked.

Ryan got up and rolled out of bed, his body facing away from her as he pulled on his pants.

"There's been another murder in Manhattan Beach," he said quietly, "in the same house as the previous killing actually. Decker wants me there now."

There was something in his voice she found unsettling, though she couldn't place what it was. He seemed to be struggling to keep his composure.

"What's going on, Ryan?' she demanded. "You're acting funny."

He looked over at her and she thought his eyes looked watery. He looked like he was about to reveal something, but then his expression changed and she knew he'd changed his mind.

"I'm just out of sorts, I guess. I didn't expect to be woken up in the middle of the night with this kind of news. It's not what I was hoping for."

She still felt like he was holding back but decided not to press.

"Is there anything I can do to help?"

"Thanks, but no. You should try to go back to sleep. The best thing you can do right now is take care of yourself."

"Okay," she said before asking, "Is Garland meeting you there?"

Ryan took a big glug of water from the bedside table before answering her.

"He's already there," he said, standing up.

"Pretty impressive for an old dude," she noted, unable to hide the astonishment in her voice. "That guy is full of surprises."

"He is one of a kind," Ryan agreed as he bent over to give her a kiss on the forehead. "Try to go back to sleep. I'll check in with you in the morning."

"I love you," Jessie said as she lay back down.

"I love you too," he said softly before turning off the bedside light and leaving.

Despite Ryan's admonition, Jessie couldn't get back to sleep. For the next twenty minutes, she tossed and turned but just couldn't get comfortable. Something about his demeanor when he got the call kept flashing through her mind.

When he was listening to Decker talk, Ryan had gotten an expression she almost never saw on his face. It wasn't simple shock or sadness. It was some combination that seemed bigger and more profound. And then it came to her. For a second, before he'd managed to regroup, he'd looked devastated.

She sat up. There was no way she would be able to fall asleep now. She went to the bathroom and splashed water on her face. Staring at herself in the mirror, she was pleased to see that her eyes weren't rimmed with exhausted redness. Of course, that would likely change fast if she was up for the day, as seemed to be the case.

She returned to the bed and sat back down. Her mind kept flashing to the expression on Ryan's face when Decker first started talking to him. Whatever the captain had said, something was horribly wrong.

She grabbed her phone and was about to call Garland when she thought better of it. Ryan had said he was already at the crime scene. That meant he was likely very busy and not in the mood to answer her questions. Instead she called the Central Station desk sergeant, who gave her the address in Manhattan Beach.

Without ever formally acknowledging to herself what she was doing, she started getting dressed. Five minutes later she was ready to go. She scribbled a quick note for Hannah, which she slid under the girl's bedroom door. Then she left the apartment, making sure to turn all the security systems back on remotely as she headed to her car.

She knew Ryan and Garland would be pissed when she showed up to insert herself at the crime scene. But she didn't care. Something was off. She felt it in her bones.

Even getting slightly lost, Jessie made it to the beach in no time.

During rush hour, the drive would have taken well over an hour. But at 3:30 in the morning, it took less than half that time, even with her missing the freeway exit and doubling back. The streets were mostly silent. As she approached the coast, a thick blanket of fog settled in, making each streetlight seem like a dull lantern in an isolated lighthouse. It gave the early morning a creepy, desolate feel.

When she arrived, she parked on Manhattan Avenue, just west of the pier and about a block from where her GPS said the address was. She walked briskly down to the Strand. Though she couldn't see the ocean at this hour, she could hear the waves crashing on the beach and knew it was close.

She didn't have to look hard to find her destination. Once on the Strand, even with the fog, the night sky was lit up by multiple emergency vehicles. As she approached the house, she counted at least half dozen police cars, an ambulance, and a coroner's van. The entire area around the mansion was blocked off and multiple officers stood guard, keeping the curious from getting too close.

She approached a scared, youngish-looking officer and held up her ID, figuring he'd be the easiest to get past.

"I work with Detective Hernandez," she said nonspecifically. "Can you tell me where he is?"

"He's upstairs," the officer said. Though she'd never met him, Jessie thought the kid seemed surprisingly shaken. She looked at his name tag.

"You okay, Officer ... Timms?"

"Yes ma'am," he assured her, pulling himself together. "It's just, I had met the victim. I liked him. And then I ended up being the one who found him."

"I understand," she said, giving him a gentle pat on the shoulder. "It's never easy when you have a personal connection."

"No ma'am," he said, lifting the police tape so she could duck under.

"How did you happen to find the victim in the house so late at night?"

She realized the question sounded accusatory, though she hadn't intended it that way.

"He was supposed to return the key after a few hours. When he didn't come back, I went to check on him and ..." He broke off, overcome with emotion.

Jessie wanted to ask why someone would be returning a key to the police so late at night but she could tell the kid was in no condition so she let it go.

"Thanks for your help, Officer," she said. Unable to think of anything else to say to comfort him, she turned and walked up to the house.

She held up her ID again for the officer guarding the door. He stepped aside to let her in. She glanced at the foyer floor and saw the chalk on the floor from what she assumed was the first victim. She glanced upstairs, where she could hear several voices. One of them sounded like Ryan's.

She started toward the stairs, when another officer standing at the base of them who appeared to be a sergeant held up his hand. Unlike Officer Timms, he looked older and more battle-worn.

"Can I help you, ma'am?" he asked politely but challengingly.

"I work with Detective Hernandez," she said, holding up her information for the third time.

"I'll let him know you're here," the sergeant, whose name tag read "Breem," said, not stepping aside.

"I hear his voice," she said more testily than she would have preferred. "I can let him know myself when I get up there."

"I'm sorry, ma'am. Detective Hernandez was very clear that no one was to come upstairs without his express authorization. He wants everything done meticulously on this one."

"He's like that with every case," Jessie replied forcefully. "What makes this one different?"

The sergeant gave her a perplexed expression. He opened his mouth to respond but before he could, a familiar voice called out from the second floor.

"Jessie?" Ryan said, looking down from the landing. "What are you doing here?"

She looked up at him and could tell immediately that he was upset by something unrelated to her showing up unannounced. As she stared at him, a sense of dread started to spread through her. She darted up the stairs before Sergeant Breem could stop her. The man started to follow her but she saw Hernandez shake his head.

"It's okay, Sergeant," he said.

"What's going on, Ryan?" she asked quietly when she reached him at the top of the stairs.

"I need to talk to you privately outside," he whispered.

"No. What's going on? Where's Garland?" she asked, sidestepping him and looking into the bedroom.

She blinked slowly, hoping that what she saw on the bedroom floor was an illusion. But when she opened her eyes again, he was still there. In between the coroner and a crime scene tech, Garland Moses was lying on the floor. He was dead.

CHAPTER NINE

Jessie felt her chest tighten and found that she couldn't breathe. She tried to speak but only a wheezy exhalation came out. She swallowed hard, trying to lubricate her suddenly dry throat. She reached out for the railing as she squinted at Ryan, wondering if that might somehow change things.

"I'm sorry," he said as he reached out to her.

She shook her head violently and he stopped.

"What?" she asked absently though she'd heard him quite clearly.

"Come with me," he said, taking her arm and leading her to a balcony at the end of the hall.

He turned to face her and opened his mouth but nothing happened. He closed his mouth as he seemed to struggle with how to begin. Then he tried again.

"It looks like he came back here last night to check out a lead. From what we've found so far, it appears he was attacked in the master bedroom. There was clearly a struggle. He was murdered, strangled to death."

Jessie felt her mind racing out of control and tried to rein it in. Part of her brain was already asking questions about the crime scene. But, furious with herself, she forcibly shut it down, actually squeezing her eyes closed tight as if that was some sort of internal off switch.

Garland was dead; the criminal profiler so legendary she'd been afraid to approach him at first. The man who'd eventually become a mentor to her, and later a friend she trusted with her darkest secrets, would never again tease her or test her or support her. He was gone.

Jessie felt a wave of grief wash over her even as she heard real waves in the distance. It was as if the ocean knew her pain and decided to give it a soundtrack. She bent over at the waist and instructed herself to take multiple deep breaths before trying to speak again.

When she finally felt like she had regained some measure of control over her body, she stood back up. Ryan was studying her with a concerned expression.

"I'm okay," she said, though she wasn't certain that was true. "Walk me through the scene."

Ryan stared at her like she was crazy.

"I can't do that," he said in disbelief. "You're in no condition to be reviewing a crime scene right now."

"But you are?' she demanded, feeling a sudden, inappropriate level of anger rising in her belly. "You knew him too."

"Yes," Ryan conceded. "I knew him and I liked him. But I was nowhere near as close to him as you were. And it was still brutal for me. I actually called in Trembley to help out because I was struggling with it."

"Is he in there now?" Jessie asked. Alan Trembley was the junior detective in the HSS unit at Central Station. Despite his youth, he'd proven to be an energetic and capable member of the team.

"Yes, and he's doing a great job. I'm going to tell him to take over so I can get you home."

"No," she argued. "I don't want to you to miss something important because you weren't here."

"Jessie. We've got it locked tight up there. We're not using MBPD for this investigation. The officers in there with Trembley are from our station. The deputy coroner and crime scene techs are ours. Captain Decker insisted on using all our own people and the Manhattan Beach chief didn't say boo. We've got photos being taken, video being shot. Everything that can be done is being done. Let me take you home. I'll have someone drive your car back. Trust me. You don't want to be in there."

Jessie glanced over his shoulder at the beach in the distance. The fog was starting to dissipate. She still couldn't see the water but could make out the silhouettes of several people walking on the sand.

Who would be out walking on the beach at this hour?

She shook her head in frustration with herself.

What difference does that make right now? Get your head on straight!

"Okay," she finally answered. "But let's go down there first."

Ryan looked in the direction she was facing and nodded.

"Just wait a minute," he said. "I want to let Trembley know what's going on first."

"Go ahead," she said distractedly. "I'll meet you on the sand."

Ryan led her down the stairs and then headed back up. Jessie walked out the front door and found a set of steps leading from the Strand down to the bike path below and beyond that, the beach. She took off her shoes and held them by the heels with her fingertips as she walked toward the water.

Thought it was early summer, at this hour the sand was still cool as it shifted under her feet and wriggled its way between her toes. She moved slowly so as to keep her balance, following the sound of the waves more than any visual cues. As she got closer, one of the old blue wooden lifeguard stations came into view.

She passed it and noticed that the sand was now harder and more tightly packed. A few steps farther and she felt the dampness under her feet where the tide had recently come in. The water was now visible. She watched as the waves collapsed in on each other, creating a frothy surf that bubbled white as it reached out longingly for her toes. She sat down just out of its reach and watched.

After a while—she wasn't sure how long—Ryan arrived and sat down beside her. He didn't say anything and neither did she. She reached her hand out and he took it. She leaned over and rested her head on his shoulder. She thought that maybe the crashing waves hid her weeping. But she wasn't sure and she didn't really care.

He watched until the sun came up.

At first it was hard with the fog and because he was several blocks away. But after he found a pair of binoculars in the master closet, he was able to go on the rooftop deck and keep tabs on all the comings and goings six blocks down the Strand, where it had happened.

He was weirdly excited by it all. There was something satisfying in knowing that he was the reason the beachfront was a symphony of sirens the last two nights. He didn't completely understand it. The first night made sense. But the police response in the middle of last night seemed even more intense than the night before. Maybe there was something he was missing.

Eventually, as the sun rose over the hills in the east, he retreated back into the home he'd adopted for the time being. He wanted to sleep but it was hard with all the excitement. His mind kept flashing back to what he'd done, what he'd taken away.

He'd never intended to kill that woman. After all, he was minding his own business in the Bloom house, the one they always left for weeks at a time during the summer. He wasn't bothering anyone.

But then that busybody woman from next door, with her plastic body and even faker smile, had to show up. He thought she'd go away after a while but she actually entered the house, committing the same crime he had. He hoped she'd just go and let him get back to his life. But no, she had to get curious and give herself a tour of the house. If only she'd kept her nose out of it, she'd probably be alive today.

But once she saw him, he had no choice. She likely would have given a description of him to the police and then he'd be in a really desperate situation. So he had to stop her, had to silence her. He couldn't let her take away the lifestyle he'd been living, even if it was only temporary.

So he'd strangled her. Initially, he was riding on adrenaline when he slammed her against the door and later, wrapped the stocking around her neck. There was a moment, when she was really flailing and struggling, that he briefly had second thoughts. Maybe he could just knock her out and make a run for it, go somewhere else entirely.

But then the old fury reared its head. Why should *he* have to leave to accommodate the desires of another rich bitch? He'd done enough of that in his life. Suddenly he was squeezing her neck even tighter, imagining she was one of the models who used to do whatever he wanted but wouldn't even look at him now. He watched the stocking material dig into her flesh, cutting off her circulation, and felt a thrill of almost orgasmic excitement at the realization that her life was literally in his hands.

And then it was over. She lay limp on the floor. The buzz started to fade almost immediately. He tried to keep his head about him, aware that the woman's husband didn't usually get home for at least another hour.

He hurried around the house, wiping down every surface he could remember touching. He'd worn gloves virtually the entire time he'd been there. But one could never be too careful. Within fifteen minutes he was ready to go. He borrowed one of Bloom's sweatshirts, pulled the hoodie over his head, and left. No one gave him a second look.

Now, as he rested on the bed in his latest unsanctioned Airbnb, he recalled the feeling he'd gotten as he stole the last bit of life from that woman. It wasn't something he'd ever have thought himself capable of. Yet he had to admit, it was a rush unlike anything he'd ever experienced. And if he was honest with himself, it was something he'd been longing for ever since. He knew it would happen again. The only question was when.

CHAPTER TEN

Ryan made coffee while Jessie showered.

Neither of them even considered going back to sleep once they returned to the apartment just after five. Hannah would be up in an hour anyway. The realization crushed Jessie anew.

How am I going to tell her?

Her sister wasn't known for expressing her emotions or even necessarily having them. The concern that Hannah was a narcissistic sociopath incapable of feeling empathy was something Jessie had discussed with Garland on many occasions.

Now that worry would be put to the test. Hannah and Garland had become friendly, maybe even close, to the extent that was possible for her. Would she feel gutted by his loss? Or would it just be one more body in the endless parade of death she'd faced in the last year?

First her adoptive parents had been killed in front of her. Then the same thing happened to her foster parents. She'd seen Jessie tortured. She'd watched a serial killer murder a man in an attempt to co-opt her into becoming one herself.

And now this, the murder of a man she viewed as a paternal figure, who listened to her and took her seriously. At what point would she just shut down, too numb to the horrors she'd seen and suffered to engage with the world? Had it already happened? Was she just faking normal emotions?

When Jessie emerged from the bedroom, she found she would be able to test that question right away. Hannah was up, wearing a bathrobe and sipping coffee on the couch. When Jessie glanced over at Ryan, he shook his head imperceptibly to let her know he hadn't said anything about what happened.

"Morning," Hannah mumbled when she saw her.

"Morning," Jessie replied as casually as she could.

Hannah cocked her head to the right, a probing look on her face.

"What is it?" she asked.

"Huh?" Jessie replied, feigning confusion. She needed more time to prepare for this.

"Something's up," she said with certitude. "You're being fake cheerful and Ryan's doing everything he can to avoid making eye contact with me. What's going on?"

Jessie walked over, trying to think of how best to broach the subject. She sat down next to the half-sister she hadn't known existed less than a year ago. Hannah stared at her with an odd mix of expectant trepidation. She'd learned to almost smell bad news coming.

I owe it to her to be honest. She's earned that.

"I've got bad news," she said slowly. "I had hoped we were done with saying that for a while. But I guess we're not."

"What do you mean?"

"Garland Moses was murdered last night while working on a case," Jessie answered without hesitation.

Hannah's face went from apprehensive to blank almost immediately. It was as if she was intentionally doing a forced shutdown of all her essential systems right there on the couch. She said nothing.

"I don't know a lot about what happened yet," Jessie continued, uncomfortable after the long silence. "But we're going to get to the bottom of it. In the meantime, I thought you should know. He liked you and I think you were fond of him too."

Hannah seemed to reboot. Her eyes, vacant a moment ago, fixed on Jessie. She didn't seem angry or upset or scared. She was present but not much more.

"He was nice," she said quietly, without expanding on it.

"He was," Jessie agreed. "I'd grown to lean on him quite a lot recently. After I lost my adoptive parents, he was the closest thing to a paternal figure I had. And now I've lost him too. I'm pretty raw right now."

"Yeah," Hannah said flatly. "It's kind of hard to process it actually."

Jessie glanced over at Ryan, who was still standing at the kitchen counter. He gave her a reassuring nod.

"It really is," she agreed. "When this is all over, I was planning to make an appointment with Dr. Lemmon to talk it out a bit. Would you like me to make one for you too?"

"Can I think about it?" Hannah asked. "Right now I just kind of want to get a handle on my own thoughts, you know?"

"Sure. And if you need to take the day for yourself, that's okay. I can smooth it over at school."

"No," Hannah said. "I should go. I don't want to just sit around. It'll be good to have something to keep me busy."

Okay," Jessie said. "But if you find that it's too much, you can change your mind."

She certainly understood the urge to throw oneself into an activity to take your mind off whatever trauma was consuming you. She'd used the tactic on many occasions. But she knew it wasn't always the healthiest choice for her. And she was even more dubious when it came to Hannah.

"I will," the younger woman said. "But for now, I'm going to try to push through. In fact, I better shower and get dressed."

She got up and returned to her room, closing the door firmly behind her. Jessie looked over at Ryan.

"What do you think?" she asked.

"I think that girl is going to need therapy for the rest of her life. And even that probably won't be enough."

The station was deathly quiet. Even the protesters out front, who never seemed to tire of marching with signs claiming Jessie was a racist, seemed more subdued than usual.

In the bullpen, there was little of the background chatter that usually created a constant buzz throughout the day. Most folks were seated at their desks, quietly typing away. Others huddled in small groups, whispering in hushed tones. There was a pall over the building.

This was the first time she'd been in the station since her injuries three weeks ago. But no one gave her a second glance, not even to send her the dirty looks she'd been expecting from her co-workers after the hateful social media posts that had been falsely written in her name. Everyone was focused on the man they'd lost.

Since she wasn't scheduled to be back for another week, it made no sense for Jessie to go to her desk. Instead, she walked straight to Captain Decker's office. Ryan matched her step for step.

To Ryan's credit, he hadn't even tried to dissuade her from coming in when she told him what she was doing. He must have known it would be pointless. She was going to work this case, whether she was in pain, whether skin was falling off her back, no matter what.

She was about to knock on the door when Ryan leaned over and spoke quietly.

"All I ask is that you don't go in hot. Give Decker the benefit of the doubt. He might surprise you."

She nodded as she rapped on the door.

"Come in," came a weary-sounding voice.

They entered to find Captain Roy Decker seated behind his desk. Jessie hadn't seen him in person since he visited her at the hospital two weeks ago, the day she was discharged. If it was possible, he looked even more beaten-down than he had then.

He had his usual sunken face and wrinkled brow. His hawk-like nose still protruded prominently. But his normally sharp, piercing eyes were hazy and red. And his tie had been loosened so that it dangled, almost like a necklace, around his white dress shirt. For perhaps the first time since she'd met him, he had on no sports jacket. She could tell he'd been up all night. He looked a decade older than his sixty years.

"How are you, Hunt?" he asked gently, making no mention of the fact that she wasn't supposed to be here.

Jessie wasn't sure if he was referencing her physical status or her emotional reaction to Garland's death. She knew Decker was aware that the two profilers were friendly. But she doubted the captain knew just how close they'd gotten in recent months. She decided that revealing that might be detrimental. He was less likely to let her get involved if he thought it was too personal for her.

"I'm okay," she said, without getting specific. "I'm here to help."

"How's that?" he asked.

"Garland Moses was killed while investigating a murder. You need someone who can step in and find out who killed both that woman and him. I work with Detective Hernandez all the time. I'm the natural fit to take over."

Decker stared at her, his eyes growing sharper by the moment.

"Just stepping up to do your professional duty, huh?" he asked skeptically.

"No, Captain. You know it's more than that. Yes, Garland Moses was a friend of mine. Of course I want his killer brought to justice. But even if I'd never met the man, you can't deny that I'm the best person to take over this case. He was the best profiler on the West Coast, without question. But I'm no slouch. I work in the same station. I regularly deal with the detective handling the case. I know Moses's habits and instincts. I'm the best person to pick up where he left off."

Decker didn't respond at first. Instead, he looked at his computer screen as he clicked his mouse. Jessie glanced over at Ryan, who shook his head slightly, to indicate that she shouldn't push any farther. After several more seconds, Decker looked up.

"I can tell that you're physically not one hundred percent. It looks like you're afraid your own shirt is going to rub your back too hard. How am I supposed to put you back in the field?"

"I've got Mr. Six Pack Abs with a brain here to protect me," she said, nodding at Ryan. "And I promise to take it easy."

"You never take it easy, Hunt," he replied. "That's why you're on leave in the first place."

"And that's why this is the perfect time to put me on the case. I'll be so reluctant to cause myself discomfort that there's no way I'd put myself in harm's way."

Decker sighed deeply.

"You understand that putting you on this doesn't mean I buy a word of your crap, right?"

"Of course, sir," she said, fighting back a smile. "May I ask why you are putting me on it?"

"Because you did say one thing that's true—you *are* the best person to pick up where Moses left off. In fact, he always told me that when he retired, he felt comfortable knowing you would be around to pick up the slack. We're about to find out if he was right."

Jessie was filled with two emotions she didn't know could exist concurrently: pride and fear. She was proud that Garland had that kind of faith in her. But she was terrified that she was going to let him down. The mix was so confusing and overwhelming that she rushed out of Decker's office without another word. As she left, one phrase kept repeating on a loop in her brain.

He's counting on you.

CHAPTER ELEVEN

The morgue had never felt so cold.

Jessie had been here many times, but never to examine the body of a friend. She found it difficult to separate her personal connection to the victim from her need to focus on the details of his death.

They were waiting in the adjoining room for the coroner to bring them in. As they did, Jessie looked through Garland's personal effects in the plastic bag Ryan had given her. There wasn't much, just a watch, his glasses, and his notepad.

"They don't need this stuff for evidence?" she asked Ryan.

"Everything's already been processed," he told her. "There was nothing noteworthy. Even the notes on his pad were hard to decipher. Maybe you can make something of them."

Jessie nodded and put the pad in her pocket to review later. Then she turned to face the man she loved.

"We have to catch this guy," she insisted. "Not just for Garland. This is two murders in two nights. Who knows what he's got planned for tonight? So fill me in."

"You've read the report," Ryan said. "Details are pretty sparse. The husband's been eliminated as a suspect. The homeowners were out of town. Despite what Priscilla Barton thought when she entered the house, there was no one renting the place. The MBPD canvassed the neighborhood and came up empty. No one saw anything out of the ordinary. Of course, this is a community in which people ambling around from house to house isn't cause for much concern."

"Yeah, well, forgive me if I don't trust the interrogation skills of cops from a sleepy beach town. I think you and I should re-canvass all the neighbors. Maybe they just haven't been asked the right questions."

"I'm all for that," Ryan agreed.

Jessie continued, barely listening to him.

"And we need to find out what's going on with the killer," she said. "What was he doing in that house the second night? It's pretty brazen to go back to the scene of the crime like that. Was he staking it out and saw Garland enter? Did he follow him in? Was he already there, waiting?"

"All good questions," he said. "I say we go back to the beach for the answers as soon as we're done here."

Before she could respond, the coroner waved them in. They stepped through the door. As cold as the waiting room had been, this one was plain freezing. They walked over to the exam table where the coroner was waiting.

"Are you going to be okay?" Ryan asked when she turned away from the sheet-covered form on the table in front of them.

Yeah, in just a sec," she assured him, trying not to hyperventilate.

After a few seconds, she turned back and nodded at him.

"Go ahead," he said to the deputy medical examiner, who pulled back a white sheet to reveal Garland's lifeless body.

The first thing Jessie noticed was just how frail he looked. In his standard slacks, dress shirt, and sports coat uniform, it was easy to overlook. The man had projected authority and mental strength. But Garland Moses was a small man, maybe five foot eight and 150 pounds. His skin was weathered and wrinkly and his chest was slightly con-cave. His body seemed so insubstantial compared to what he had accomplished.

Jessie noticed something else too. He was covered in scars, including what looked like healed-over bullet wounds. Having studied his career in detail, she knew he'd been in Vietnam and won a Purple Heart for injuries suffered in a firefight in 1969. She also knew he'd had several "up close and personal" run-ins with violent killers over the years. But she'd never seen the physical accumulation of all those encounters laid out so plainly. She couldn't help but wonder if one day, someone would be looking at her body on a metal table, studying the map of disfigurement that her body was fast becoming.

"I never realized just how much he'd been through," she said quietly.

"Yeah," Ryan agreed. "A detective who retired a few years ago told me Garland was asked to give a lecture when he first started consulting for the department. It was mostly an overview of the basics of behavioral analysis. But apparently people just kept peppering him with questions about his past cases. They wanted to hear his war stories. This retired detective told me that Garland mentioned that he got an exit physical when he left the FBI. The nurse counted up all his various scars and wounds. There were fifty-seven. And that was prior to any of the cases he handled for LAPD."

"Jeez," Jessie muttered.

"The detective said Garland didn't give any more lectures after that."

Jessie studied several of the deep marks that ran along both of the man's upper arms. They looked meticulous and intentional.

"I wonder how many of these are from his run-in with the Night Hunter," she mused.

The Night Hunter was a notorious serial killer that Garland Moses had pursued while in his last years at the FBI. The killer had murdered and dismembered over fifty people up and down the eastern seaboard for a decade.

When Garland closed in on him, the Night Hunter got the upper hand, captured him, and tortured him for two days before Garland finally got free and fought back, using the man's own machete against him before the killer ran off into the night. Garland managed to get to a hospital and recover.

The Night Hunter was never found but the murders stopped after that, so many in law enforcement believed he died that night. Garland still thought the guy was out there, but that didn't stop him from retiring a month after getting out of the hospital. He never spoke of it to Jessie.

"I'd say at least half of them," Ryan said, jolting her out of her thoughts. "He's got a series of carvings in his back from the guy, like some grotesque artwork. I would have thought he might have tried to have plastic surgery at some point to clean them up."

Jessie looked over at him and shook her head.

"We profilers keep the scars as keepsakes," she told him, her voice filling with emotion at the renewed realization that Garland Moses was done with reminders. "So we don't get too comfortable."

"I wonder what kind of keepsakes he kept of his wife," Ryan asked.

Garland's wife, Gloria, had died nearly forty years ago from breast cancer, when he was still new to the FBI. She was only twenty-seven. They hadn't had kids and he'd never remarried. Jessie never even heard of him going on a date in the intervening years. None of that information came directly from Garland, who rarely spoke of those days.

"Those keepsakes are internal," she said softly.

There was a slight cough from the medical examiner, who was standing there quietly, waiting to give his report.

"Go ahead," Ryan said.

The guy began methodically listing off the injuries that Garland had incurred last night.

"He has bruising on his upper back, a fractured right hip, torn skin on his forehead, a hematoma on the back right portion of his skull, and a crushed trachea. It looks like almost all of those occurred during the course of the struggle. The actual cause of death was asphyxiation as a result a wide, leather-based item, almost certainly a belt."

"Are you sure? I thought this guy used a stocking," Jessie noted.

"The woman was killed with a stocking," Ryan inserted. "But it looks like things got changed up here."

"Can we account for the source of all the injuries?" Jessie asked.

Ryan nodded.

"Trembley worked with the tech team and CSU to put together a meticulous recreation of events that I think makes a lot of sense," Ryan answered, pulling up the report on his phone. "They used audio from the smart speaker in the bedroom, along with clothing fibers, blood spatter, and carpet markings. He thinks Garland was at the wife's dresser when he was surprised by the assailant. They struggled and he was knocked backward into the dresser, explaining the bruising on his upper back. They think he broke his hip when he either fell or was pulled to the ground. The trachea is explained by the belt, as is the damage to the forehead skin. It seems the attacker was on top of him, with Garland lying on his stomach. The only injury they couldn't account for was the hematoma on the back of his head. They assumed the attacker smashed the back of his head down on the ground at some point but there was no blood or hair on the carpet and no carpet fibers in his hair. Trembley thought that Garland might have initiated the contact, maybe using his head as a weapon to break free."

"That actually fits," the examiner said. "He does have some neck strain than doesn't seem connected to the belt strangulation. It looks almost like whiplash. If he was throwing his head back in an intentionally violent way, then that could account for the strain."

"It sounds like he was a fighter to the end," Ryan said admiringly.

Jessie was turning over ideas in her head. After a moment, she responded.

"I'd like to think that's the case," she said. "And maybe it is. But I'm not sure."

"What do you mean?" Ryan asked.

Jessie closed her eyes, picturing the struggle, imagining Garland on the floor with a broken hip, a belt around his neck, and a man straddling him from above.

"It's true that he could have been fighting to get away," she acknowledged. "But Garland wasn't a man known for false hope or dramatic gestures. He had a broken hip. He wasn't going anywhere. He had to know he was going to lose this fight. So maybe he wasn't trying to get away. Maybe he was trying to help us catch his own killer by branding him with evidence of the fight."

"How?" Ryan asked curiously. He'd known Jessie long enough not to be dismissive of her theories, no matter how out there they were.

"I'm not sure. But maybe we should ask the MBPD to make a note of any local residents with bruises on their faces and forward them to our team. I know it's a long shot but I feel like Garland was trying to leave us one last clue."

Hannah couldn't focus.

It didn't help that she'd already read *Wuthering Heights* twice on her own and the lecture her English teacher was currently giving captured none of the romantic torment that made the story so compelling. Ms. Gorton made the stormy battles between Catherine and Heathcliff seem somehow bland; the tortures they inflicted on each other rote.

Of course that wasn't the only reason she was having trouble paying attention. She couldn't stop thinking about Garland Moses. She couldn't help but imagine him lying cold on some metal table, his eyes forcibly closed by some flunky who thought it might bring him peace.

Garland was a really decent guy. She liked how he never patronized her or treated her like she was some frail, damaged bird. He teased her. He called her out on her crap. He took her seriously. He genuinely seemed to care about her welfare. But unlike Jessie, he wasn't so close to her situation that he inadvertently smothered her. As Hannah sat in class, using Ms. Gorton as a kind of human white noise, she realized something surprising: she would miss him.

It was surprising because she had come to learn that she didn't typically react strongly to loss. Even before her adoptive parents were murdered, she noticed that she wasn't as emotionally fazed by traumatic events as others. She was pretty good at faking it when she heard about a school shooting or a baby beaten to death by his stepfather or thousands dying in an earthquake. But she rarely ever felt more than the mildest form of something resembling pity.

When her parents were killed, she felt emotions for sure—terror in the moment, confusion at what was going, a sense of loss of normalcy in the weeks that followed. But she wasn't sure she ever felt true grief at their loss. She wasn't even sure how that emotion would manifest itself.

She'd seen it enough on television that she was able to model it at their funeral. And in the months that followed she was able to play-act at something approximating mourning. But it never felt real to her.

She wasn't proud of it. In fact, she kind of hated it about herself. It made her feel apart from everyone else in the world. She sensed that some people were aware of it—Jessie, Dr. Lemmon, and Garland—even if they didn't address it with her directly. She wished she could change it.

She actually tried in recent months, especially with her sister. Despite Jessie's flaws, of which there were many, Hannah sincerely liked her. She was funny and tough and whip-smart. She was one of the few people who could relate to what Hannah had been through. She had experienced variations of the same traumas herself so she wasn't just blowing smoke when she talked about getting it. And she seemed to be honestly trying to be a good big sister to her, to give her some kind of normal home life. Hannah appreciated that.

When she thought of Jessie, a pleasant sensation of affection came over her. She wished good things for her in her work, in her relationship with Ryan, in life. But would she grieve if Jessie was murdered by a killer tonight? She wasn't sure. She'd miss her, just as she missed Garland. But was that the extent of it?

Before she could ponder the question more, the bell rang. She gathered her things and headed to lunch. As she walked distractedly down the hall, letting routine guide her along the familiar path, the desire to probe her own psyche faded. She allowed her mind to slowly refocus on the present and her surroundings.

The moment she did, she got an odd prickling sensation, like when superstitious people say someone has stepped on their grave. She stopped and looked around the campus courtyard. There was nothing unusual, just "troubled" teenagers wandering to their various classes and clubs and like her, to lunch.

And yet she couldn't shake the strange sensation that she was being watched. She'd faced far too many real threats to simply dismiss the feeling as an overactive imagination. Once again, she scanned the courtyard, looking for anyone or anything that seemed out of place. But nothing jumped out at her. Still, she stayed alert as she continued to the cafeteria. The tingling didn't stop until she was halfway through with lunch.

CHAPTER TWELVE

The beach looked less welcoming this time.

As Ryan drove them back to the crime scene so that she could get a sense of the place in daylight, Jessie sat in the passenger seat, letting her mind wander. She stared out the window at the crowds of people who had staked out spots on either side of the Manhattan Beach pier for as far as the eye could see. Whereas last night the beach had seemed almost empathetic, today it looked intimidating.

It was a hot, muggy day. When they left downtown, the temperature was in the mid-nineties. But even here by the ocean, it hadn't dropped much. The dashboard readout said it was eighty-seven.

They parked in the police station lot a few blocks from the water, mostly because there were no available spots on the street. Even though it was a weekday during work hours, the town was packed. They walked the two blocks west to the Strand along the main drag on Manhattan Beach Boulevard. Jessie couldn't help but glance at the storefronts.

They were a mishmash of overpriced beachwear boutiques, crowded outdoor cafes, pressed juice bars, tiny art galleries, and tourist shops that sold everything from scented candles to lingerie to kitschy wooden signs that said things like "This way to the beach→."

Everyone around her was having a great time, but Jessie could feel her chest tightening with anxiety. It took her a second to realize why. This community reminded her of Westport Beach, the wealthy, coastal Orange County community ninety minutes south of here that had briefly been her home only a few years ago.

She had never felt truly comfortable there, even before her ex-husband tried to kill her. The gaudy McMansions, overly inquisitive neighbors, and sour "grass is greener" mentality left her feeling lonely and depressed for months before she figured out that moving there was part of Kyle's elaborate plan to lead a life of consequence-free decadence. When she got in the way of that, she became expendable. But almost from the start of their time there, she *felt* expendable.

As they reached the bottom of the steep boulevard, where the shops gave way to a parking lot dominated by surfers changing into and out of their wetsuits, she pushed the memories from her mind. This was *not* Westport Beach. It was a different community and she needed to be careful not to let her biases against the one bleed into her analysis of the other.

Ryan glanced over at her and seemed to sense her disquiet.

"We don't have to go straight to the house," he reminded her. "Why don't we walk down to the end of the pier, just to clear our heads? As long as we're here, we may as well take in the view."

She nodded without replying and they wandered to the end of the pier, hand in hand. There was a small aquarium at the very end, in a quaint building with a Spanish tile roof. It bore a sign that said it had been there since 1920, an eternity in Los Angeles time. They walked past it, careful to steer clear of the men casting their fishing rods nearby until they got to the very end of the pier.

They could see sailboats in the distance and massive cargo ships in the haze beyond that. Just south of the pier, a line of patient surfers waited for their perfect swell. Just to the north, the water was comprised mostly of swimmers and boogie boarders, happily riding even the smallest waves. She could hear little kids squealing with pleasure while they tried to outrun the water that chased them back up the beach.

"How are you doing?" Ryan asked.

"I'm trying to remember that there's beauty in the world, even on the darkest days."

"How's that going for you?"

"Right now, pretty well," she said. "I'm going to try to hold on to this mental picture."

"Me too," he said, smiling at her.

She smiled back but when she spoke, her words were firm.

"Let's get to work."

It took a moment before Jessie felt clear-headed enough to actually investigate.

She was standing in the Blooms' bedroom, almost in the exact spot where her friend and mentor had taken his last breath. Ryan's head was down, reading something on his phone.

Without his eyes on her, she allowed the grief to consume her for just a moment. Her knees buckled slightly. She felt a catch in her throat. But then, as quickly as the feeling had come, she pushed it aside. She'd deal with it later. Right now she had work to do.

She alternated between looking around the room and studying the cryptic words on Garland's notepad. He seemed to speak a language only he understood. The words on the page were English but they were barely legible and rarely formed coherent thoughts. Instead, the last page was comprised of individual words and unfinished phrases, among them: "OTB," "missing h," and "fetish?"

She glanced up again, imagining the bedroom at night, trying to picture the circumstances of the attack.

"You said there were no security cameras, right?" she asked.

"Right," Ryan confirmed, reiterating what he'd mentioned on the drive over. "The Blooms didn't have any. They had a smart speaker in the corner over there. As I mentioned, the tech team took it and checked the audio. It helped verify the time and some details of the attack. But no one actually spoke. It was mostly banging, grunts, and moans."

Jessie tried not to think about that. She was glad she hadn't heard the thing.

"What about neighbors?" she asked. "Any of them have cameras?"

"Some of them do," Ryan told her. "But none have angles that clearly show this house."

Jessie nodded, wondering how likely it was that the lack of footage of this home was a coincidence.

"Can you stand just outside the bedroom door?" she asked him as she stepped over to Gail Bloom's dresser.

Ryan stepped outside and turned back to her. She turned to face the dresser.

"Okay," she continued. "Now walk slowly toward me, as quietly as you can."

She closed her eyes as he approached. After about five seconds she heard the creak of a floorboard and whipped around. Ryan was less than six feet away.

"That must have been what tipped Garland off," Ryan noted. "But by the time he heard it, the guy was almost on top of him, too late to do anything."

Jessie agreed. She turned back to the dresser where her mentor had been standing less than twenty-four hours ago. He had to have been facing this way to have been taken so unawares. What was consuming his attention to the point that an attacker was able to get so close without him noticing?

She opened the top drawer. It was filled with women's underwear, bras, and a few pairs of workout ankle socks. It looked like they'd been quickly rifled through. She wondered if that was what Garland had been wondering about. Had Priscilla Barton's killer had some kind of fetish for stockings and been in here with them when he'd heard the neighbor come in the house? Maybe that was what the reference to "missing h" meant—Gail Bloom's missing pantyhose.

If he was up here, ogling the homeowner's underwear, that meant he hadn't invaded the home after Barton arrived. He was already here. He had already made himself comfortable.

As Jessie tried to recreate what Garland had been thinking last night, she began to get into a rhythm. It was like she was having a silent conversation in her head with Garland, asking him questions that his actions and notes attempted to answer.

The effect it had on her was both reassuring and troubling. One part of her was comforted. This interaction with his mind and memory brought her closer to him. But it also made the pain of his loss, of knowing they'd never interact this way again in life, all the worse.

"I think we've got all we can from the house for now," she said suddenly. "Maybe we go outside and talk to some neighbors?"

"Sure," Ryan agreed.

Once outside, they decided to split up to cover more ground.

"Just remember," Ryan said delicately, "one of these folks might be our killer. You're not in any condition to take someone on right now. So please don't go into anyone's house. Invite them outside to talk. Better to be curt than caught."

"Did you just make that up now?" Jessie asked.

"I did. What do you think?"

"I think they should teach that at the academy," she teased. "You really missed your calling, Shakespeare."

"Hey, you know I'm a sensitive soul," he countered, pretending to be wounded.

"All right you. Take your sensitive soul and go south. I'll take the houses that head north toward El Porto Beach."

Ryan faux-pouted as he stomped off dramatically. Jessie went in the other direction, skipping the home of Garth Barton. She knew he was at work now but she'd been warned to steer clear even if he was around.

The next hour was instructive even if it didn't move the investigation forward as much as she would have hoped. Jessie learned from multiple residents that many locals rented out their homes for part of the summer while they went on extended vacations.

"Technically, it's a municipal violation to do that without jumping through a series of administrative hoops," a middle-aged guy three doors down from the Blooms told her. "But many folks do it on the down low, skirting regulations and making off-the-books deals.

"The problem," he continued, "is that when something untoward happens, whether it be a theft or just a noise ordinance violation, there's no formal record of who is staying in any given house or where to reach the homeowner. It makes enforcement challenging."

Worse, according to some, it changed the "vibe" of the community. One retired widow described it in coded terms that made Jessie squirm uncomfortably.

"Suddenly our charming beach town gets overrun with strangers, and not just the ones expected during the day when the masses swarm the beaches. But also in the evenings, when leisurely evening strolls lead to encounters with people who don't value the 'specialness' of the community."

"It really sucks to go to the local coffee shop in the morning and not recognize half the people there," one irked, forty-something bleached blonde woman wearing a massive diamond ring said obliviously. "It detracts from the homey feeling I like."

Jessie got a distinct NIMBY sensibility from almost everyone she spoke to. Sometimes there was a racial undercurrent. But other people seemed to want to keep the place clear of anyone who wasn't local, no matter where they came from.

She could feel the angst rising in her again. Even though most people she interviewed were pleasant, chill folks who simply enjoyed the slower pace of living by the beach and walking around their neighborhood barefoot, there were the others. Approximately every third interviewee reminded her of the people who made her Orange County existence so fraught.

Part of why she'd chosen to live downtown was because even the wealthy folk there embraced a kind of grittiness that felt more real than the plastic lives of these people, living in their cookie cutter mansions and worrying that they might encounter an interloper in the line for coffee.

She reached the last home before Bruce's Beach, a park which served as a kind of informal dividing line before the next stretch of homes. The closest mansion was a good hundred yards farther north and it seemed unlikely that anyone that far away would be of much use as a potential witness. She decided that after this house, she'd turn around.

The place was set farther back from the Strand than many of the others. It had an actual, full-sized yard with a beautifully landscaped garden than ran on either side of the walking path to the front door. To get to that door, she had to open the wooden gate and walk up a series of uneven pavers. She felt very exposed, especially so far from the Strand and its constant crowds.

She knocked and waited, marveling at the work it must take to keep the yard in such immaculate shape. She was tempted to walk around the side of the house to see just how far back the foliage went. But just then, the door opened to reveal a thirty-something man with a burly chest and an even burlier belly. He wore board shorts, a loosely buttoned Hawaiian shirt, and a thick, gold necklace that disappeared under the shirt. She wouldn't have been surprised if it dangled all the way down to his navel.

"Yeah?" he said by way of greeting.

"Hi. My name's Jessie Hunt. I consult with the LAPD, which has been brought in to help investigate the recent deaths in your neighborhood. I was hoping I could ask you a few questions."

"Some cop already came by yesterday," he said, sounding somewhere between agitated and surly. "I already told him we don't know anything. He said this all happened on Monday night, early evening, right? We were on our boat out of Redondo Harbor then."

"Yes, sir," she said non-combatively. "We appreciate those details and we're running them down. Of course, there was more than one death."

"But I heard the other one was in the middle of the night. How am I supposed to give you proof of an alibi when I was asleep?"

"We're not asking for an alibi at this time, Mr....?"

"Jules. Cory Jules."

"Okay, Mr. Jules," Jessie continued. "As I said, right now, I'm not trying to lock down resident alibis so much as get a feel for the area. My understanding is that during the summer, there are a lot of extra renters."

"That's an understatement," Jules muttered. "I can't keep track of the East Coast usurpers who come out here every June to muck the place up. If it's not them, it's an army of entitled fraternity brothers who want to see if they can break the Guinness record for keg stands or some Wisconsin tractor company owner and his five kids with cheese coming out of their pores."

Jessie didn't comment on the irony of the rotund man in front of her commenting on someone else's weight or sense of entitlement. Instead she tried to refocus him.

"I'm wondering if you noticed anything that wasn't so much annoying as out of the ordinary," she said. "Did you see anyone recently who was behaving, not obnoxiously, but more … suspiciously?"

Cory Jules scratched his wild, patchy hair as he thought about the question. After a few seconds, his eyes lit up.

"There is someone," he said excitedly. "It was last week so I forgot about it. But we had to fire our gardener for peeping."

"Excuse me?"

"Yeah," Jules said, obviously enthused to be retelling a story he'd shared more than once. "It was last Thursday, I think. My wife, Peg, said she was changing in the house and she saw the gardener—I forget his name—looking at her through the window. She didn't want me to call the cops and make a scene. Instead, she had me call the landscaping company—they do a lot of homes here on the Strand. They fired him the same day."

"And you think this man is capable of something as involved as a murder?"

"I don't know," Jules said, though it sounded like he believed it. "But I could imagine him peeping at Priscilla Barton. She had a pretty hot bod and she liked to show it off. If he got caught doing that sort of thing a second time, I could see him worrying that he might get more than just fired. Maybe he'd get arrested. I could see him wanting to shut her up in a moment of panic. It doesn't seem crazy to me. But you're the cop."

Jessie didn't correct his misimpression. Instead she asked for the name of the landscaping company, which he went back into the house to get. As he walked down the hall, Jessie saw who she assumed was Peg Jules poke her head out briefly. In that short moment, Jessie saw something unsettling in her eyes. Fear? Apprehension? Whatever it was, it was clear that there was more going on here than met the eye.

A moment later, Cory Jules returned with a bill in his hand. Jessie wrote down the company's name and phone number. As she thanked him, she studied him closely. But as before, he looked like just another coddled, self-righteous beach dude.

If he was something more nefarious, he was doing a great job of hiding it. And if he was that great an actor, what else was he capable of?

CHAPTER THIRTEEN

They were a long way from the beach.

As they headed inland, Jessie watched the temperature gauge in Ryan's car slowly creep up. But as the temperature rose, her spirits sank listening to Ryan describe his interviews with neighbors. They yielded stories similar to hers but nothing concrete to advance the investigation.

By the time they arrived at the Boyle Heights home of Carlos Fogata, the temperature was approaching a hundred degrees. They had gotten his address from Beach Cities Landscaping, which apparently maintained the yards and gardens of nearly a quarter of the homes along the Strand.

When Jessie called, the company proudly informed her that they had a staff of eighty-six. So it was likely no big deal for them to fire Mr. Fogata, the Jules' primary gardener. And it may have explained why they let him go without any kind of administrative review of the merit of the allegation. As Shelly, the perky public relations liaison Jessie spoke to, said, "We don't take chances when it comes to alienating the community."

They pulled up to the address Shelly had given them and stepped out of Ryan's air-conditioned car into the sweltering midday heat. They were standing in front of the Shady Palms Mobile Home Park, just a few miles east of their own downtown police station. They approached the park's main office, where the on-duty manager gave them the lot number where Carlos and May Fogata lived.

As they trudged along the dirt path that served as a road, the dust rose up all around them, sending Jessie into a coughing jag that made her body shake and her back sting. When she recovered, she pointed at the dead trees that stood forlornly at random locations.

"Not much truth in advertising," she noted. "Those aren't palms and they're not very shady either."

Ryan smiled wryly.

"I have a feeling that most folks who live here long ago made their peace with the incongruity of the name and the reality. I know I did."

"What do you mean?" Jessie asked.

"My family lived in a mobile home for three years when I was a kid. At one point there were six of us sharing a space smaller than your apartment living room. I still remember the smell of grilled onions on the stove and playing football outside, using different trailers as yard markers. They're some of the best memories of my childhood."

"You never told me any of this," Jessie said.

"Well, considering your upbringing, I didn't think mine was especially hardscrabble."

"Ryan," she said reproachfully. "It's not a competition to see who had the most challenging childhood. I'm just happy to get a peek at the little fella behind that manly facade."

Ryan's face was suddenly bright pink and not because of the sun.

"It looks like we're here," he said quickly as they arrived at the Fogata home, knocking before she could reply. A moment later the door was answered by a petite woman in her early thirties with her hair pulled back in a bun. She was drenched in sweat.

"Is Carlos here?" Ryan asked. "We'd like to speak with him."

The woman nodded and called into the home for Carlos. He appeared a few seconds later, wearing blue jeans and a white T-shirt, which was soaked through. He looked slightly older than the woman, maybe mid-thirties. He had the lean body and leathery skin of someone who worked outside all the time. His hair was starting to recede and he had little scratches and scars on his fingers and wrists that Jessie recognized as the telltale defense mechanism of rose bushes. He wore a worried expression.

"Hi, Carlos," Ryan said. "I'm Detective Ryan Hernandez with the LAPD. This is my colleague, Jessie Hunt. Do you have a moment to answer some questions about an incident that occurred last week in Manhattan Beach?"

Fogata's concerned look immediately turned to annoyance.

"Let me guess. Is it related to Margaret Jules?"

"It is," Ryan confirmed. "May we come in?"

Fogata gave them both a once-over.

"With that suit you have on, I think you'd rather we talk outside. We don't have air-conditioning. You'd be cooking in your own juices in that thing."

"I appreciate it," Ryan said. "Maybe you could lead us to the coolest spot?"

"Give me a second," Fogata said, disappearing from sight.

Ryan didn't flinch but Jessie did notice him snap the holster cover off his weapon and rest his hand casually in its general vicinity. But when Fogata reappeared, the only thing he'd added was a Dodgers baseball cap.

He hopped down from the trailer and motioned for them to follow him as he walked up a small hill to a picnic table in the middle of the park. There were a couple of preschool-age kids sitting there, drawing pictures on construction paper with worn down crayons. Fogata plopped down next to them and motioned for Ryan and Jessie to take seats across from them.

"These are my twins, Joe and Mariah," he said, rubbing the boy's head vigorously. "They'll be four next week."

Jessie smiled at the kids, who looked at her with matching expressions of mild curiosity before returning their attention to their art.

"You okay having this conversation with them around?" Ryan asked.

"I've got nothing to hide," he assured them. "And as long as you're not too graphic, they won't have a clue what's going on. Besides, this is the only place in the park that gets a breeze and I don't want to make them move."

"Fair enough," Ryan said. "So you're obviously aware of the complaint filed by Ms. Jules last week."

"Obviously," Fogata confirmed. "That's why I'm sitting here instead of on the job today. Did you guys really come all the way out here from the beach just to question me over an 'incident' she wouldn't even file a formal police complaint about?"

"You say 'incident' like it's a dirty word," Jessie said, speaking for the first time.

"No, I say it like it's a load of crap."

"You're saying it didn't go down that way?' Ryan asked.

"Not even close, man," Fogata said. "That lady has been eyeing me for months."

"What does that mean?" Jessie asked, though she had a clue.

"It means she was constantly giving me the look. She always found a way to end up sunbathing in the yard while I was working. It got so awkward that I requested getting switched off their house. But the company said no, that Mrs. Jules was adamant that I did the best work. After that, I never even stepped on their property without sunglasses and a hat that covered the top half of my face. I tried to avoid eye contact at all costs. I didn't want any trouble."

"You're saying she came on to you?" Ryan said.

"Not flat out in direct words, man. But she was always getting in my personal space, squeezing my hand when she thanked me, inviting me inside for a glass of lemonade. I know that sounds like she was just being polite. But half the time she was in a bikini. And she never did it when her old man worked from home, only on days when he was at the office. How convenient is that?"

"What about last Thursday?" Jessie asked.

"Right. So the husband's off at work. The kids are at school. And she does her regular routine, this time deciding she's gonna do some outdoor yoga right as I'm trimming the hedges. I do my standard thing—covered face, sunglasses, headphones—pretending not to notice her bending into a pretzel ten feet from me. Then I go around to the side of the house to cut back the ivy along the walls. I'm on the ladder near a second-floor window that looks into one of the kids' rooms. I take off my hat and sunglasses for a second to wipe the sweat out of my eyes. And guess what I see?"

He paused, apparently waiting for them to actually guess. Just then, a hot gust of wind blew lazily across the park. To Jessie, it felt like someone was using a hair dryer on her back. She grimaced silently. Though it offered no relief, it was strong enough to send Mariah's artwork flying off the table. Carlos snatched it in mid-air and delicately placed it back down in front of his daughter.

"Why don't you go ahead and tell us, Carlos?" Ryan prodded.

"Okay. She's in the room, pulling off her sports bra, right in front of the window, staring at me like I'm a lollipop she wants to lick. And remember, this is her kid's room she's changing in, not her own. She could have picked any room in the house. But she goes to that one, stands right in front of the window, and waits until I'm looking that direction to pull her top off."

"What did you do?" Jessie asked.

Carlos half chuckled as he recalled the moment.

"I almost jumped off the ladder right then even though I was a dozen feet up. I scrambled down, left the rest of the ivy to do what it wanted. I got my stuff and moved it around front. I was almost done at that point anyway, so I just cleaned up. I was getting ready to leave when she came out. She was dressed normal then, shirt and pants. She asked if I wanted the check. I said yes. She said she forgot it inside and could I follow her to get it. I told her I was in a rush to get to my next job and I'd pick it up next time. That was a lie. She was my last job of the day. But I had to get out of there. I gave her a forced smile and said goodbye. But I could see from her face that she wasn't happy. She looked embarrassed and pissed. So I wasn't surprised when I got the call later that night. They fired me, no questions asked, no chance to defend myself, just done."

Jessie thought back to the expression she'd seen on Margaret Jules's face earlier and realized she'd misidentified it at the time. It wasn't fear or apprehension. It was guilt.

"Why didn't you report what happened?" she asked. "Just to get ahead of it?"

"Are you kidding, lady?" he demanded incredulously. "I'm supposed to go into the office and call out a customer for flashing me? You think they'd believe me? Even if they did, you think they'd care? They probably would have fired me for complaining, just because I was more trouble than I was worth. My only hope was that she'd be too ashamed to say anything. I should have known better."

Ryan and Jessie exchanged a look. Neither was anxious to broach the main reason they were there. But since Ryan had done most of the heavy lifting so far, Jessie decided it was her turn.

"So did you go back at all afterward, maybe to pick up a final check from the company?"

"Yeah. I went back but not for a check. They stiffed me on that, said I violated some morals clause and I was lucky they didn't report me to the police. But I had to wash and return my uniform and turn in the key to the truck I used."

"When did you do that?" Ryan asked.

"The next day—Friday."

"And you haven't been back since?" Jessie pressed.

"No," he said slowly, clearly sensing something else going on. "Why?"

"Because we're not here about the allegation made by Mrs. Jules," Jessie said. "We're here about a series of murders that occurred earlier this week. Did you hear about those?"

"I haven't been keeping up with the news lately. But one of my buddies from the job told me a body was found in a house just off Sixteenth Street. Is that what you're talking about?"

"Yes, Carlos," Jessie confirmed. "But it wasn't just one body. It was two different people on consecutive nights in the same house. One of them was a local woman. The other was a man who worked for the LAPD. So we're following up on every lead. And when we heard there might be a Peeping Tom in the area, we had to check it out. You understand that?"

"Sure, I guess."

"Great," she continued. "Do you know Priscilla Barton, Carlos?"

Fogata appeared to search his memory.

"I don't think so, at least not by name."

"What about Charles and Gail Bloom?"

"I know those are the people who own the house where the body, er, bodies, were found. But that's only because my buddy told me that."

"Does Beach Cities Landscaping work on their home?" Ryan asked.

"Yes. But I don't usually. I maybe helped out there a couple of times in the last year. Besides, they'd cut back on landscaping while they were gone. No one had been there in a few weeks."

"So you knew they were out of town?" Ryan wanted to know.

"It was common knowledge."

"Did you have a key to their place?" Ryan pressed.

"No," Carlos said, sounding offended, his voice suddenly hard. "But that doesn't get me off the hook, Detective. There was nothing to stop me from getting a copy made at a hardware store on a day when I did work there. Are you about to read me my rights?"

Jessie ignored his indignation.

"Do you know a man named Garland Moses?" she asked, an edge in her voice.

Fogata shook his head.

"It doesn't ring a bell."

"Where were you Monday, Carlos, late afternoon to early evening?" Ryan asked.

The man's head was swiveling back and forth, trying to keep up with their volley of questions.

"I was stuck in a two-hour traffic jam, driving back from Agoura Hills."

"Why were you there?" Jessie demanded.

"Job interview. It's an even longer commute than to the beach but I'm in no position to be choosy."

"Did you get it?" Ryan asked.

"I'm still waiting to hear."

"We'll need the phone number and the name of the person you met with," Jessie told him.

Fogata sighed.

"What's wrong?" she asked.

"What do you think it'll do for my job prospects if a police detective calls them up to ask if they can confirm I was there in order to rule me out as a murder suspect?"

Ryan looked at Jessie, who suddenly felt mildly ill. No matter how this played out, it looked like Carlos Fogata was going to get screwed.

Or maybe not.

"Did you have your phone with you that day?" she asked.

"Yeah."

Jessie turned to Ryan.

"Maybe we can find another way to confirm Mr. Fogata's alibi without contacting the folks he interviewed with."

Ryan looked at her with a mix of bemusement and admiration.

"I was not expecting that," he said before turning to Fogata. "Carlos, assuming this info checks out, we might be able to rule you out as a double murderer. This could be your lucky day."

"Man," Fogata said, shaking his head ruefully, "as much as I appreciate that, I gotta say, I haven't had a lucky day in four years."

Jessie believed him. More importantly for her work, she was becoming increasingly aware that her natural skepticism toward rich beach folk wasn't based in unfair bias but in hard-won experience. It never hurt to be reminded that she was dealing with a bunch of vipers, especially when she was about to return to their pit.

CHAPTER FOURTEEN

"What do we have left for snacks?" Agent Poulter asked from the driver's seat. As the senior agent he got to choose whether to drive or ride shotgun.

Agent Cress leaned back and rifled through the cooler in the backseat. Another pitfall of being the junior agent was that he had to stock the supplies each morning.

"We're down to Sun Chips, string cheese, and juice boxes."

"No water?" Poulter wondered.

"We used it all up. But at least these will give us a sugar hit."

"I always crash after the juice," Poulter complained. "Just give me a string cheese."

"Your system is falling apart, old man," Cress replied as he reached back to find the cheese, ignoring the rivulet of sweat that streamed down his back toward his backside.

Agents Poulter and Cress were uncomfortable. They'd heard rumors that one or both of them might soon be pulled off the Kyle Voss surveillance detail. But as of now, they were both still sitting in their black Hyundai Elantra across from his townhouse, blasting the air-conditioning in the ninety-four-degree heat of Claremont, California.

The overnight team was jealous of them, because they got to go home to their families each evening and sleep in their own beds. That was certainly true. But the night guys didn't spend all day sweltering in a metal box, trying to avoid detection even though Voss was clearly on to them.

No matter how many times they changed vehicles or their stakeout location, he made a point of waving at them every time he drove by. Then they had to follow him as he drove all over Southern California, attending meetings, having lunches, and doing interviews. They had lost him on more than one occasion, though they were later able to confirm his whereabouts.

Both agents were hopeful that the whole detail would be pulled. There was no way one agent could handle the alternative, solo duty, with the need for food and bathroom breaks, not to mention driving around while coordinating with support staff.

Both were confident it would happen by the end of this week. It might have been different if they found something, but they hadn't. Since getting out of prison, Voss had been a Boy Scout. Neither of them bought the act. The guy was a murderer. He'd killed one woman and then tried to kill his own wife. They were also sure he was in deep with the Monterrey-based Monzon drug cartel. But they couldn't prove it.

His phones were tapped but he said nothing suspicious. There were cameras in his house but he did nothing out of the ordinary. They had a tracker on his car but he didn't go anywhere unexpected. He'd led a straight-arrow existence, at least for the last three weeks. And unless he did something problematic in the next two days, they would likely have to cut him loose.

But at this moment, both agents were both more interested in snacks than surveillance. Cress had just snagged a piece of cheese for himself when his partner gave him a whack on the arm.

"Hold up," Poulter said. "It looks like we have movement."

Cress let go of the food and looked in the direction his partner was pointing. Voss lived in the back unit of a two-home townhouse. They saw a car emerge from the garage, ease down the long driveway, and turn right, away from where they were parked.

As he drove off, the driver waved at them through the open window. He didn't seem to be trying to lose them so Poulter didn't rush as he made a U-turn and began following the target.

Kyle Voss sat on the couch, watching the FBI agents on his extra phone as they drove off.

He knew the FBI had attached a tracker to his car, a blandly gray Toyota Prius. But in doing so, they had missed the small, web-enabled camera he'd installed in his back seat. The resolution was so good that he could see clearly through their windshield and knew when they were talking, making a phone call, eating, or even picking their noses.

When they were a couple miles away, he got up and went to the bathroom of the house he was in. Of course, it wasn't his house but the one that backed up to his backyard. What the FBI didn't know was that before he even bought the townhouse, his friends in the Monzon drug cartel had purchased both townhomes on the adjacent lot, one street over.

In the weeks leading up to Kyle's release from prison, they dug a tunnel from the back townhouse on that lot, underneath the wooden fence separating the two backyards and into the guest bathroom of the townhouse Kyle eventually bought. The tunnel mouth opened into the cabinet below the bathroom sink.

As the cartel expected and Kyle confirmed after moving in, the FBI did not put a camera or bug in that bathroom, only the master upstairs. As a result, he was able to climb through the tunnel opening, crawl along it underneath the connected backyards and emerge in the laundry room of the house one street over.

He'd been doing it regularly for weeks now. The first time he'd gone over, he met the resident of that home, a man who went by "Rick" and who just happened to be a dead ringer for Kyle. They even took measurements to be sure.

Rick was slightly smaller than Kyle. At six foot one and 210 pounds, he was an inch shorter and five pounds lighter. But he had the same muscular build and their subtle physical differences would be lost on almost everyone. Their facial bone structure was similar, though Kyle's nose was slightly more petite. The folks in Monterrey had considered having Rick get a nose job but decided the recovery time would be a complication, a risk not worth taking.

He had dyed his hair the same shade of blond as Kyle's and shaved it to the same length so that both men were growing it back at the same rate. Rick had brown eyes but wore blue contacts outside the house just to be safe, even though he usually wore sunglasses everywhere.

He'd purchased the same wardrobe as Kyle and made sure to get sizes that gave the same snug fit. On the several occasions when Rick took the tunnel to Kyle's house and left in his car, the outings had gone without incident. He made sure to wave at the agents as he left, though he always tried to pull out of the driveway in the opposite direction from them so they couldn't get too good a look at him.

On this day, Rick was off to run a series of errands that wouldn't require him to interact with many folks. He had Kyle's regular phone so the FBI could keep tabs on his location. He was going to the nearby Claremont Colleges Honnold/Mudd Library to "read" a few textbooks to bone up on new finance regulations. Then he would make stops for gas and to the grocery store. Depending on what Kyle needed to do and how long it might take, Rick could make the trip plausibly last between two and four hours.

In the bathroom of the other townhouse, Kyle changed into appropriate attire for his planned outing, hopped in the Toyota 4Runner in Rick's garage, put on his cap and sunglasses, and pulled out of the driveway, past the front house, which was also owned by the cartel and currently unoccupied.

He looked both ways for safety and to confirm that there were no FBI agents on that street. When he felt comfortable, he pulled out of the driveway and headed toward his intended destination, confident that he was free to do what was needed.

CHAPTER FIFTEEN

Kelly Martindale was pissed.

She had spent a good ten minutes circling the streets of downtown Manhattan Beach, looking for anywhere to park. Exclusively residential streets needed permits. All the public lots were full. And there were no available meters other than the twenty-four-minute ones. She needed a lot more than twenty-four minutes.

Finally she saw a woman walking out of a boutique with both hands holding shopping bags and followed her slowly, basically stalking the chick until she got to her car, three blocks south of the main drag. She was pretty sure the woman took an extra-long time loading up just to spite her.

When she left, Kelly pulled in, paid the meter up to the two-hour maximum, and hurried down to Carl's place. When she got to his massive mansion on the Strand, three blocks south of the pier, she was torn.

It was only six minutes until their planned meeting time and she wanted to be ready when he arrived. He'd been in New York since last week and was returning today. He'd told her he wanted to ravish her as soon as he got home.

But she also needed to be discreet. After all, Carl Landingham was married and Kelly was his mistress, not his wife. It was true that Mrs. Landingham—or Mrs. Landinghag, as Kelly called her—was out of town all week. But that didn't mean the neighbors wouldn't talk if they saw something juicy.

So despite both her urge to rush in and the sultry afternoon weather, Kelly pulled the hoodie on her sweatshirt over her head, strolled casually to the house's side door, and used her spare key to get in. Once in the house, she moved fast.

She hurried up to one of the three guest rooms, where she changed. It was safer to do it in a rarely visited room, in case someone unexpectedly came over. She could stuff her clothes in the extra closet or even hide in the room if need be.

She undressed quickly, stripping out of the sweatshirt, top, and leggings. Then she pulled the lingerie out of her small backpack. Carl usually liked her to wear something elaborate. But considering the heat, he'd recommended she go with a light, silk teddy. She did as he asked but added a little something extra—a pair of sheer, thigh-high stockings she knew he'd enjoy rolling down her legs when the time came.

Kelly looked at her watch. It was exactly 1:29. Carl would be here any second. She rushed into the bathroom to give herself one last check and was immediately glad she had. Her long, black hair was still in a ponytail. She pulled out the tie and let her hair cascade down past her shoulders.

Under normal circumstances, she'd brush it out. But she didn't have time and it looked sexy in casual, blowsy way. Everything else looked good. The teddy hugged her hourglass figure in all the intended places. The stockings ran up her long legs teasingly. Even before she put on the pumps, she knew she was bringing it today.

She was under no illusions about the nature of their relationship. Carl had taken an interest in her because she looked good at the lingerie fashion show where they'd met three months ago. It didn't take long after that first meeting for him to find out what was under that lingerie or for her to get the spare key or the other perks that came along with it. But she was well aware that if she wanted to keep her human slot machine dropping coins, she needed to keep him happy.

It wasn't that much of a burden anyway. While Carl was nearly thirty years older than Kelly, who had just turned twenty-three, spending intimate time with him wasn't objectionable. He was good looking, in a distinguished, *Scent of a Woman*–era Al Pacino kind of way. Kelly loved that movie.

And he was in solid shape for a man his age, a result of what she knew was a pretty intense workout regimen. In fact, he'd lost a few pounds since they started spending time together, which she attributed to his desire to impress her.

Sometimes she imagined that he'd leave his wife and she could finally stop sneaking around. But Carl had warned her that if Mrs. Landinghag ever found out about them, the party would be over. Apparently, despite his job as a television executive, she was far richer than him. It was her house. She owned three of their four cars and their boat. She leased the private jet that currently had her spending an extra week in Manhattan.

But all those were worries for another time. Once Carl arrived and they got reacquainted, she could move her car into the garage until his wife returned. She could lounge around the house naked if she wanted. She could lie out on the beach or borrow Carl's boogie board. It was like she would be on vacation, even though her tiny Culver City apartment was only a dozen miles away.

She giggled excitedly at the thought of it as she made her way down the long hallway to the master bedroom. She was just about to walk in when she heard what sounded like a soft groan. Or was it a snore? Unsettled but curious, she peeked around the corner and saw someone sleeping in the bed, turned away from her.

She was slightly startled by the sight. Had Carl already arrived? Why hadn't he called to tell her? And couldn't he stay awake long enough to see her? That hag of a wife must have really worn him out for him to crash in the afternoon.

She decided to sneak over and give him a wake-up surprise. Tiptoeing over as carefully as possible while wearing stilettos, she made her way around the bed. Carl had the covers over his head. Kelly carefully grabbed hold of them, ordering herself not to laugh and ruin the prank, and then ripped them off the bed completely.

The man startled into consciousness, looking up at her with initially sleepy eyes that suddenly opened wide with shock. It wasn't Carl. Kelly screamed, first in fear, then in embarrassment as she stumbled back, nearly losing her balance.

For half a second, as her heart dropped into her stomach, Kelly wondered if she was in the wrong house. But she dismissed the thought immediately. This was the right home. It was hard to confuse with any others. And her key had worked.

She toggled between fear and confusion, afraid of this random dude in Carl's bed but not wanting to overreact. She tried to be logical. Had Carl invited a friend to stay while he was gone and forgotten to tell her? It wouldn't be unlike him. He was absent-minded and she knew he had lots of buddies from out of town that he let crash at his place. And this guy was clean-cut, decent looking, and wearing silk pajamas. He certainly seemed to have made himself at home.

She gulped hard, trying to regroup and hide her embarrassment.

"I'm sorry," she said quickly. "I thought you were Carl. I had no idea he had a houseguest."

The guy eyed her from head to toe, taking in her skimpy outfit, heels and all. He didn't look drowsy anymore. She suddenly realized how exposed she was and her embarrassment doubled.

"I'm just going to go back to the other room and wait there," she said as he started to sit up. "No need to get out of bed. Again, I'm really sorry for the mix-up."

She turned and hurried toward the door.

"Wait," he called out.

She turned around, hugging herself as if that might offer some kind of modest cover.

"Yes?"

"I love your stockings."

"Thanks," she said, unsure if she should continue this awkward conversation or just leave. Finally she asked, "How do you know Carl?"

He stood up and stretched. As he did, she realized that the pajamas he wore were Carl's. Strange to wear someone else's bed clothes.

"I have no idea who that is," he lied, the sleep now completely gone from his eyes.

For a moment, Kelly's brain short-circuited. This man said he did not know Carl. But he was in his house, praising her pantyhose. Kelly felt a cold shiver run up her spine. And then, when the man began walking quickly toward her, she screamed.

She turned around and ran as quickly as she could down the hall to the top of the stairs. But as she reached them, her left heel broke. She lost her balance and began to tumble. She threw up her arms to try to protect herself but it didn't help.

The momentum sent her slamming into the side wall like a pinball and then across the stairs into the balusters on the other side. Somewhere along the way she hit her head hard. By the time she got to the bottom stair, she was disoriented and sure she'd broken some part of her left leg.

Ignoring the confusion, pain, and the sound of the footsteps coming down the stairs behind her, she grabbed the handrail and tried to pull herself upright. She was almost standing when the man caught up to her and pushed her to the floor. She landed heavily on the marble and found that she was unable to get up. She felt woozy and weak. The man walking toward her looked blurry.

She tried to crawl away but found that her right arm wasn't working properly. Then he was on her, pinning her down as he pulled the stocking off her right leg, the one that wasn't bent in an unnatural direction. Then he moved up so that he was sitting on her ribcage. He took the stocking, wrapped it around her neck twice, and began to squeeze.

She tried to yell for help but only a hoarse rasp came out. Until now, she'd been so desperate to escape that the fear hadn't fully taken hold. But now it did. Despite the agony of her multiple injuries and the feeling of drowning that being choked caused, she was overcome with sweaty clamminess as terror overcame her.

She shook her body wildly in the hope that it might dislodge her attacker but he didn't seem even slightly fazed. She tried to scratch at his eyes with her working hand but he appeared oblivious, merely closing them.

She sensed the strength leaving her body and looked around for anything to defend herself. One stiletto rested just feet away from her. But it was on the same side as her broken right arm. Besides, she didn't think she had the wherewithal to swing it, even if she could have grabbed it.

As her vision got blurrier, she thought she was hearing things. A loud metallic sound rang in her ears. It was strangely familiar. And then, in a flash, she knew it was real. The sound was the garage door opening. Carl was home. But then, in what would be her last fully formed thought, she realized something else: he wouldn't get to her in time.

CHAPTER SIXTEEN

An hour and a half after leaving Carlos Fogata, Jessie and Ryan were back at the beach.

She was glad that he didn't mind driving because she was over it. Besides, the trek allowed her to get in a much needed nap. The only downside was that when she woke up, she discovered that she'd been slumped backward and her top had adhered to her back. Peeling it away from her raw skin without screaming out loud was an accomplishment.

After parking at the police station, they made their now-familiar walk back to the Strand. As they did, Jessie thought about Cory Jules, the homeowner who'd demanded Carlos be fired. She wondered if his squirrelly demeanor was an indication of something more than just being an entitled jerk.

She found it hard to believe that a guy with his physical proportions could move stealthily around the Bloom house without being noticed by neighbors. She found it even harder to imagine that he could get the jump on Garland, who was older but still a very alert, reasonably spry guy. Though she didn't completely dismiss him, she thought they needed to look at other possibilities and Ryan agreed.

"Maybe we should talk to some folks south of the pier," she suggested. "It seems like everyone in this area knows each other. Maybe someone in that direction noticed something unusual. I don't think we need to just stick to the couple of blocks near the crime scene."

"Good point," Ryan said, smirking slightly. "We can see if the people on the other side of Manhattan Beach Boulevard reveal their nosiness and prejudice differently than their friends to the north. I wonder if they consider themselves to live on the wrong side of the tracks."

"Very funny," she said as they walked along a stretch of the Strand she hadn't visited before. "Should we split up again?"

"I don't ever want to split up," he said, smiling goofily.

She knew what he was doing. Ryan was trying to take her mind off the fact that she was exhausted, sore, and weighed down by grief. It wasn't entirely working but she appreciated the effort.

"Then let's start out together," she replied.

They began knocking on doors. Since it was still early afternoon, they didn't get many answers.

"I wonder how many of these people are at work and how many are just out of town," Ryan mused.

"Either way, it makes our job harder," Jessie muttered.

After three failed attempts, they came to the front unit of a massive, fancy, four-unit condo complex. There was no need to knock on the door because the apparent owner of the beach-adjacent unit, a sixty-something man wearing only shorts, was sitting out front on a wooden bench, holding what looked like a massive margarita. His skin was deeply bronzed and crinkly and the white hair on his chest formed tight little curlicues.

"No trespassing," he growled as they approached, though he appeared delighted to see them.

"Getting started on the evening early?" Ryan asked, nodding at the man's drink.

"How do you know I ever stopped?" he asked grumpily, before looking at Ryan's suit and adding, "You're wasting your time. I don't want to be saved."

"We're not actually here for that," Jessie said, trying not to be charmed by the gruff disdain the guy seemed to have for them. "We're with the LAPD, investigating the deaths up the way. I assume you've heard about them."

"Do I seem like the kind of guy who would have heard about them?" the man asked before taking a generous sip of his drink.

"Actually, you do," Jessie assured him. "May I ask your name?"

"May I ask yours?"

"Of course," she replied sunnily. "I'm Jessie Hunt, a criminal profiler for the department. This is Detective Ryan Hernandez."

"Jessie Hunt," the man said, playing with his silvery goatee. "I know that name. Aren't you the gal who wrote all that crap about your cop bosses on Facebook and got crushed for it?"

Jessie was surprised. Most people fixated more on the hacked racist and anti-Semitic comments falsely attributed to her than the ones where she supposedly called her superiors corrupt.

"That would be me," she conceded.

"Too bad it turns out you didn't really write them," he opined. "It would have been fun to watch the crap fest that could have played out in public if you really had called them out."

"It's been a pretty sizable crap fest despite the comments being faked," she told him before trying again. "So what's your name?"

He looked like he was going to continue to be combative, but then seemed to change his mind.

"My full name is Randall Horatio Fuller. But my friends call me Randy. My enemies call me Full-Of-It."

"Do you have a lot of enemies, Randy?" Jessie asked playfully.

"I sure do. I'm kind of a one-man neighborhood watch around here. And as it turns out, my neighbors don't take too kindly to being watched."

"Seen anything interesting lately?' Jessie asked, fully aware that he was dying to share everything he knew.

"You could say that," he replied, making a token effort to be coy.

"Why don't *you* go ahead and say that," Ryan suggested.

"Well, here's the thing, Detective Hernandez," Randy offered. "It's real easy to pick out the troublemakers in the wintertime around here. Everybody's living in their own homes, leading their normal lives. It gets chilly, so you don't get all the inlanders coming down. And it gets dark earlier so anybody out and about when they shouldn't be draws notice. But the summer's a different story altogether."

"How's that?" Ryan asked.

"For one thing, you got all the rabble-rousers coming in from the city, looking to blow off steam. They go crazy, bugging folks who are just relaxing on the beach, getting in the way of surfers and then getting pissed when a board knocks 'em in the head."

"They should know better," Ryan said, egging him on.

"*You* get it," Randy said, before glugging some more margarita. "Those types are bad enough. But what's worse is when residents take off for the summer. Some of them leave their places unattended and the yards get all gross. That's a whole other story. Then there are the folks who rent out their places. Now, all of a sudden I have to deal with a different breed of rich troublemakers who think they own the town, treating the locals like crap and the streets like their own personal garbage dump."

"Sounds like a real nightmare," Jessie offered, trying to sound sincere.

"It is," Randy agreed enthusiastically. "And then I get the worst of both worlds."

"Like what?" Ryan wondered.

"For example, there's this couple that lives two doors down, Carl and Eileen Landingham. She's the worst so I don't mind when she's gone, which she is right now. But Carl—who's not actually a terrible guy—he's got this chippy he likes to bring around when Eileen's away. The girl has no regard, playing music too loud, that kind of thing. Carl thinks he's being all sneaky but everybody knows what's going on."

"Sounds rough, Randy," Jessie said, feeling that she'd buttered him up enough to get more specific. But before she could ask her real questions, Randy's eyes went wide. He pointed behind them.

"Speak of the devil," he said, looking at a fifty-something man who was sprinting out his front door, yelling and flailing his arms wildly. "That's Carl there now."

Jessie and Ryan looked at Carl, who appeared to be in genuine distress. Then they heard what he was screaming.

"Help me! Someone killed her!"

CHAPTER SEVENTEEN

R yan reached the man in moments.
     He glanced back and saw that Jessie, with her still-sensitive back, was a few seconds behind.

"I'm a police detective," he said to the man. "What's going on?"

The man had an expression that was part horrified and part disbelieving, as if he couldn't process what he'd just seen.

"I just got home and found my ... girlfriend in the foyer. She's dead. Somebody did something awful ... it looks like she was beaten or something. I tried to help her. I thought she might be alive because she's still warm. But there's no pulse."

"Take us in there now," Jessie said, short of breath from just arriving.

The man ran back inside and they followed him. The door was open. Before they even got inside, Ryan could see the body on the floor of the foyer. It was rough. The victim, a woman who appeared to be in her twenties, was lying on her back, wearing nothing but a teddy. Her left leg bent back grotesquely in the wrong direction. Her right arm was equally disfigured. She was bleeding from somewhere on the underside of her head, a crimson pool slowly spreading outward.

But none of that was what drew Ryan's attention. Wrapped around her neck was a stocking, one that looked similar to the one that had been used on Priscilla Barton. Ryan noticed something else. On the marble floor were bloody footprints headed off in the direction of the back of the house. The prints were of bare feet and they looked fresh.

"I think this happened in the last few minutes," he said, looking over at Jessie. "I'm going to follow the prints. Will you call it in and secure the house?"

Jessie nodded and he took off, running down the hallway where the blood trail went. It led through the kitchen to a door that opened onto the alley. He unholstered his weapon and carefully peeked outside. The prints, now fading, headed to the right and he moved in that direction.

After about twenty yards the bloodstains disappeared completely and he was left guessing which direction to go. The guy could have hidden in any of these places, especially since so many were currently unoccupied. He looked around for any clue that might help.

Ryan was in an alley that divided the homes directly on the Strand from those one block east. They were equally impressive, in some case more so. The owners seemed to compensate for being a block away from the beach by being even more ostentatious in house size. Unlike the Strand homes, which had little yard space, the ones he was looking at now had large green spaces.

In fact, just up the way, he saw that one home with a yard had a small cabana. He squinted to make sure he wasn't imagining it. It looked like the cabana door was slightly ajar. He moved in that direction and scaled the wooden fence without any trouble. As he approached the cabana, he considered calling Jessie but didn't want to make any noise that might tip the attacker off.

When he got to the door, he saw that it was dark inside. The windows were curtained and there were no lights on. He took off his sports jacket and tossed it on the ground. For what he was planning, he'd need as much deftness as possible and wearing the jacket would interfere with that.

Without pausing to think about it too long, Ryan got a running start and dove into the room, rolling into an elegant somersault and popping upright. He spun around, training his gun on the interior of the cabana.

It was sparsely decorated with nowhere to hide. Despite the dimness, it quickly became clear there was no one in the room. Then he saw the other door. He gathered it led to either a bathroom or closet. Either way it was closed.

He shuffled to the right and approached the door from the side, briefly debating whether to try to access the room with stealth or force. But it didn't take long to decide. If someone was behind that door, they surely heard him enter the cabana.

He also doubted, though he couldn't be sure, that the killer was armed with a gun. In his experience, if someone was a stabber, they carried only a knife. If they were a strangler, they usually only had a cord, or in this case, a stocking. Most killers were quite loyal to their weapon of choice.

Still, he decided kicking in the door was wiser than trying to open it quietly, especially if it was locked. So he reared back and slammed the base of his shoe into the handle, which snapped off as the door flew open. Ryan leapt in, his eyes darting everywhere.

It was indeed a bathroom. But other than a toilet, a small, glassed-in shower and a sink, it was empty. He was about to leave when he sensed it more than heard it—the presence of another person in the cabana. He was just swiveling around when he heard the heavy breathing of someone very close by. Before he could fully spin back to the door, a body slammed into him.

As he felt the breath violently escape his chest, he flew backwards and his body smashed into the glass pane of the shower stall.

The first floor of the house was clear.

Just to be safe, Jessie had cuffed Carl Landingham to the banister in the foyer as she searched the massive mansion. Assuming he hadn't killed the girl, she felt bad about leaving him there, trapped with the dead body of his alleged mistress. But she didn't have much choice.

When she reached the top of the stairs, she saw the snapped-off heel of one of the victim's stilettos. Leaving it where it lay, she continued down the hall, checking each room. Most looked undisturbed. On the bed in one guest room, she found a small backpack. Spread out next to it on the bed were clothes that she assumed belonged to the girl, including yoga pants and a hooded sweatshirt.

Jessie left them there and continued down the hall, going room to room, until she reached the master bedroom. Unlike the others, it was clear that this room had been used recently. The bed was unmade. There was a plate with crumbs on the side table closest to the balcony. On one dresser, a man's clothes were neatly folded with a pair of sneakers on the ground in front.

Jessie left and headed back down the stairs to the foyer. She could hear the sound of sirens close by, not a shock since the department she'd called was only six blocks north. Carl was sitting on the bottom step with his head resting on his non-cuffed hand. The pool of blood around the woman's head had now expanded and was seeping under her shoulders.

As Jessie took the last few stair steps, she noticed something she hadn't picked up on in the mad dash earlier. While one stocking was wrapped around the girl's neck, she was still wearing the other one. That was different than the situation with Priscilla Barton at the Bloom house, when it seemed that the assailant had found the stocking in the dresser. This time he'd just used what was available. And yet, upon initial inspection, it looked like both stockings used were similar styles and brands. Was this the killer's thing?

Something about the sight made her recall the notes scribbled on Garland's pad. She remembered his chicken scratch saying "fetish?" Was that a reference to the use of the stocking? Then she remembered another note, "missing h." It seemed reasonable to guess that the "h" referred to hose, as in pantyhose. But what did he mean by "missing"? And she still had no idea what the term "OTB" meant. Jessie realized that another visit to the Bloom house was likely in order.

The sirens were right outside now. Jessie holstered her weapon as a precaution, pulled out her ID, held it above her head, and looked at Carl, who seemed oblivious to the noise.

"When they come in," she yelled at him over the din, "don't make any sudden moves."

He didn't look likely to make any moves at all. In fact, she wasn't even sure he'd heard her. His only priority seemed to be making sure not to look at the once-beautiful dead girl on the ground just feet away from him. She couldn't really blame him.

Her ears became overwhelmed by the endless sounds of sirens blaring only yards away. As she stood there, waiting for the cops to burst in, a random thought entered her head, one she tried not to let control her. Ryan hadn't checked in.

CHAPTER EIGHTEEN

Ryan covered his face with his arm as glass rained down on him from above.

When it subsided, he opened his eyes. He was still gasping for breath when he realized his attacker was right in front of him. He started to point his gun in the assailant's direction but his foe smashed it away with a powerful forearm.

The gun left his hand and hit the shower stall floor. He wanted to reach for it but couldn't risk it as the attacker was now on top of him, pinning his chest down with one arm as he jammed a forearm into his throat. As Ryan struggled to break free, he got his first look at the person trying to kill him.

It was clearly a man, one Ryan judged to be larger than himself. But discerning any other features was complicated by the fact that the man was wearing a black mask over his head, which had only small slits for his eyes and mouth. Making identifying him more difficult was the additional problem that he was being choked to death.

Ryan was a strong, well-built guy, but whoever this person on top of him was, he was bigger and just as brawny. Ryan punched at the man's arms but the guy seemed oblivious. He gripped the man's forearms and tried to rip them away so that he could wriggle loose. But the man barely seemed to budge. If Ryan couldn't think of something fast, he was going to suffer the same fate as Garland Moses and the women in those mansions.

He was just starting to feel panic set in when he heard sirens, loud and close. He saw his attacker, dressed all in black, perk up at the sound as well. Ryan took advantage of the man's half-second of inattention to smash him in the upper chest with an open palm.

It wasn't the hardest blow ever but the guy winced audibly and he involuntarily shrunk back. Ryan didn't wait, swinging his other arm, fist closed, upward. He made contact with his attacker's jaw. The man fell backward, his body toppling off Ryan's and onto the bathroom floor just outside the shower.

Ryan looked back for his gun. It was in the corner of the shower, mixed in with a heap of shattered glass. He reached for it anyway, grabbing it by the grip and giving it a little shake to free it from additional shards.

Gripping it firmly, he looked back toward his attacker, ready to pull the trigger. But the man was already up and scrambling out the bathroom door. Before Ryan could fire, the man disappeared from sight.

Ryan got to his feet, ignoring the slivers of glass that embedded in his hands as he pushed off the stall floor. He hurried out of the bathroom into the cabana, which was empty, and then out the door into the yard.

He saw that the larger man had already scaled the fence and was running south along the alley, away from where they'd found the dead woman. Ryan chased after him, holstering his gun as he prepared to climb the fence again. But as he reached up to grab the top of the pickets, he felt a sharp pain in his upper back.

He hopped back down and looked over his left shoulder, where he saw a shard of glass sticking out of his skin just above his shoulder blade. Reaching back with his right hand, he yanked it out, trying to ignore the searing sensation that nearly made his knees buckle.

He tossed the glass to the ground and looked back in the direction where his attacker had gone. But now the alley was empty. He considered trying to leap over the fence again but quickly decided it was a waste of time. The guy was gone. He'd be better off returning to the crime scene and giving the local cops a description so they could start a search.

Frustrated, and with his shoulder throbbing, Ryan returned to grab his sport jacket from just outside the cabana door. As he trudged over, a woman opened the sliding door to the main house and shouted out to him.

"Who the hell are you?" she screamed.

Ryan sighed deeply. Trying to keep his irritation in check, he reminded himself why he was here: to protect and to serve. When he was sure he could keep his tone calm, he forced a smile onto his face and reached for his badge. As he did, a sour thought entered his head.

I thought the beach was supposed to be relaxing.

It took several minutes to get Carl Landingham calm enough to talk. It was made doubly challenging by the fact that Jessie still hadn't heard from Ryan.

Focus on what you can control.

She had taken Carl to the breakfast table, far from the dead body. But it was only now, after half the MBPD had arrived and locked everything down, that he was finally starting to speak. He looked nervously at the uniformed officer who had accompanied them to the kitchen, as if the man might shoot him at any moment.

"It's okay, Mr. Landingham," she lied soothingly. "The officer is here for both our protection. Now why don't you tell me what happened while it's still fresh in your mind?"

Landingham nodded but still didn't speak. Jessie thought she was going to have to prod him again when he unexpectedly began.

"Her name's Kelly. She's not my wife. I was seeing her secretly. She's a lingerie model. We'd been getting together for a few months. I just got back in town from New York. She was going to meet me here at the house to welcome me back. She had her own key. I came in and was about to go upstairs because I assumed she'd be in the bedroom. But when I got to the stairs, I saw ..."

His voice trailed off at the memory. Jessie could see that he was in shock but needed to press him anyway. The longer she waited to get the details, the less she could count on their accuracy.

"You said you tried to help her because you thought she was still alive, right?"

"Yeah. When I touched her, she was warm. I thought maybe she was just unconscious. Her head was bleeding. I figured she'd fallen down the stairs. So I started to give her mouth to mouth. That's when I noticed the thing wrapped around her neck. And then I saw bloody footprints on the floor. I realized someone had done this to her. That's when I ran outside."

He stopped talking, breaking down again. Jessie nodded sympathetically and gave him a moment to recover. She glanced out the kitchen
window, from where she could clearly see the Strand. In fact, she had
a clear view of Randy Fuller, who was still sitting on his porch, sipping
his drink. The man was leaning forward, obviously watching the activity
two doors down, while trying to maintain an air of casual disregard.

Jessie was about to try again with Carl when Ryan hobbled in the
back door, holding his jacket and looking exhausted and in pain.

"What happened to you?" she demanded, standing up to help him.
He quickly waved her off.

"I'm okay," he assured her, though his voice sounded hoarse. "But I
could use a glass of water."

She got up to look for a glass but the uniformed officer stepped forward to do it. As he moved past Ryan, his eyes, wide with surprise, lingered on the detective's back. Jessie moved over to get a better look.

"You have blood seeping through the back of your shirt," she said,
hoping she sounded detached, though she didn't feel it.

"Yeah, I had a bit of an altercation. You mind if I sit down?"

She pulled out a chair and he settled into it gingerly. From behind
him, Jessie could see that he had some kind of gash in his upper back just
above his left shoulder blade. The officer put the glass of water on the
table in front of Ryan.

"Could you see if there's a medic available?" she asked the officer
before turning her attention back to Ryan. "Explain."

First he took a big glug of water. Then he dived in, explaining what
had just occurred, including his close call at the hands of a man who easily overpowered him.

"By the time I got the glass out of my back," he concluded, "he'd
disappeared from sight. I called in a description. But with all the empty
houses here over the summer, he could be hiding anywhere."

The officer returned with an EMT, who promptly removed Ryan's
shirt and began studying the wound. After cleaning it up, he got out a
suture kit.

"It could have been a lot worse," the EMT said. "I can sew it up but I recommend you go to urgent care to get it checked out when you get a chance."

"Thanks," Ryan said, clearly relieved. "I also have some shards in my palms. Do you think you could pull those out afterward?"

The EMT nodded. While he did his thing, Jessie looked outside and saw that Randy and his margarita hadn't moved.

"You mind if I check on something?" she asked Ryan. "I'll be right back."

"I'm not going anywhere," he promised. "I'll check to see if anyone's spotted my friendly man in black."

Jessie nodded approvingly, though something about Ryan's demeanor was unsettling. As she walked back to Randy's place, she realized what it was. Ryan looked shaken by the encounter in the cabana. Jessie felt a bit of fear creep into her own gut.

Almost nothing shook Detective Ryan Hernandez. If this man in black had, he must really be bad.

CHAPTER NINETEEN

Kelly's murderer, still clad in the silk pajamas, peeked out the window from behind a curtain. He was four houses south of the Landingham place but from his vantage point in the third-floor master bathroom, he could see everything the cops outside were doing.

He'd been lucky. He knew that the owner of this condo, the middle of the three massive units, was out of town. He also knew that the idiot kept his key in a fake plastic rock mixed among others just outside the door to the place. He knew that because he'd stayed in this condo before, more than once. Lastly, he knew that even in pajamas, with bloody feet, he could get here before the cops even made it out of the station.

In fact, he'd been just unlocking the condo door when he heard Carl Landingham's wail of anguish just half a block north. It was terrible and thrilling at the same time. His heart was still beating wildly at the memory of it.

As with the annoying woman at the Bloom house, he hadn't intended to kill the girl, at least not at first. After all, he was minding his own business. She was the one who'd startled him awake while he was sleeping.

After the spill she took down the stairs and his subsequent shove, he could have left. She was bleeding badly from the head and both an arm and a leg were badly broken. But she'd seen his face. She could identify him. Even then, he was on the fence. That was, until he saw the stockings.

It was like a talisman, calling out to him, telling him he had to do this. What were the chances that this lithesome young thing would be wearing the same brand of pantyhose that he'd been carrying at the Bloom house? It was as if it was all meant to be. It was as if he was *supposed* to use the stocking on her.

When he did, he felt that same buzz of exhilaration as he had the first night, only this time it was even more pronounced. He knew it was because it hadn't all happened in such a rush this time. He'd had time to consciously choose to do this. He'd been able to roll the stocking off the girl's leg, to savor the anticipation of wrapping it around her long, delicate neck.

And it was everything he hoped. As he watched the life drain out of her eyes, he felt more powerful than he ever had before, almost like a god. It was even better than the old days, when he'd actually been a man of power, a man of respect.

Despite that respect, he'd still been underappreciated by the women he coveted; the trophy wives like the one the other night, the models like the one he'd just snuffed out. Sure, they admired him. Some were even awed to be in his presence. But despite what he did for them, the contribution he'd made to their lives, none of them arrived at his place in sports bras with bottles of wine. None of them woke him up from a nap in just a teddy and stilettos.

He pictured the woman who'd put him in this position, who'd made his life what it was. She didn't look that different from the gal at the bottom of the stairs. He imagined it was her he was squeezing the life out of. As he did, he was unaware that he was grinding his teeth together.

The fantasy made him tingle all over again. That's when he accepted something he'd been keeping at bay in his mind for the last few minutes. He wanted to do this again. He had to.

Jessie stood in front of Randy Fuller, trying to get a bead on the guy. He smiled back amiably, a vague tequila haze in his eyes. The man seemed tickled to have her back.

"Lot of excitement over there," he noted, nodding at the Landingham mansion, currently swarmed by police.

"You seem very interested," Jessie replied. "Almost like you have a personal stake in what's going on."

Fuller smiled widely, squinting at her as he held up his hand to block the sun.

"Like I said, I'm a one-man neighborhood watch. I'm always interested in what happens here."

"Randy," she said, sitting down on the porch next to him. "Can I be straight with you?"

"I'd prefer it," he said, taking another big glug. The massive glass was almost two-thirds empty now.

"I think you're holding back."

"What do you mean?" he asked coyly.

"I mean, you just reiterated that you're a one-man neighborhood watch. You specifically referenced Carl when we spoke earlier, as if he was on your mind. I can't help but wonder what put him there. Care to share?"

"I feel very much under attack here, Jessie," he said, not sounding at all like he thought he was under attack.

Jessie appreciated Fuller's curmudgeonly nature but her patience was wearing thin. Time was running short and she needed answers. She decided she needed to short-circuit his buzz.

"Randy, remember how I said I was going to be straight with you?"

"Considering that you said it thirty seconds ago, yes."

"Right. So here's what's going to happen. You're going to tell me the little secret about Carl that you're guarding so preciously and you're going to tell me now. There's a dead girl in that house and I'm not in the mood to play games. If you have information that can solve her murder, I want it. If you persist in playing the role of the leather-skinned, coquettish, drunken know-it-all who keeps his mouth shut and his secrets close, you'll do it down at the station, and not this one. You'll be getting a ride to Central Station downtown, where we'll resume this discussion. After that, you'll spend the night in a cell with the guys we routinely pick up for public urination. That's where you'll sleep off your hangover, assuming you get any sleep. It's your call and you have five seconds to make it."

Randy smiled back at her, apparently impressed. But she saw a sliver of apprehension behind his eyes and knew that the answers she wanted would be forthcoming.

"I saw the girl," he admitted sullenly.

"When?"

"About ten minutes before you and Detective Hernandez stopped by. She was wearing a hoodie, thinking she was being sly, and had on a small backpack, but I recognized her. Like I said, Carl wasn't fooling anyone. She had her own key and she used it to enter the house via the side door."

"What else?"

"I saw Carl drive by while we were talking, headed to his place. He couldn't have been in the house for more than two minutes before he came running out. So if you're looking at him for this, you might reconsider. I doubt he had time to do much of anything in there."

"Is that it?" Jessie pressed.

"That's it. You still gonna drag me downtown?"

Jessie was tempted, just to see how he'd handle it. But she relented.

"You're good for now. But if I have more questions, I expect you to give me answers without attitude."

"Yes ma'am," he barked, saluting.

"Where were you by the way, Randy?"

"When?"

"In the time between when you saw the girl go in the house and when we showed up?"

Randy tried to scowl at her but his facial muscles were too tequila-loose to get the job done.

"Are you asking for my alibi? I'm an old drunk in sandals, Jessie."

"Where were you?" she asked in a tone that suggested he was in danger of returning to backtalk territory.

"I was right here," he said. "I haven't moved in an hour and don't intend to move again until this mug is empty."

She was inclined to believe him, though she gave his feet a quick glance before leaving. There was nothing resembling blood on them. And the timeline didn't fit anyway. Randy couldn't have killed Kelly, gotten back to his porch, then thrown on an all-black outfit, survived a fight with Ryan, and returned to his porch. It was ridiculous.

But as she walked back to the Landingham mansion, something about that thought reverberated in her mind. She couldn't quite put her finger on it but she knew it would make sense when she got back to the house.

Without even thinking about it, she broke into a run.

CHAPTER TWENTY

The coroner was removing the body as Jessie led the small group up the stairs.

She was first, followed by a uniformed officer, Carl Landingham, Ryan, and a second officer. She marched down to the master bedroom and walked in. It was just as she'd left it. As she looked around, the fuzzy thought that had been dancing in the back of her brain stepped forward. She waited until everyone else had filed in to begin.

"Mr. Landingham," she began, using his last name to reestablish some sense of formality now that he'd calmed down a bit. "You said that you've been out of town since last week, correct?'

"Yes," he said. "My wife and I left last Thursday. I came back this afternoon. She's supposed to return on Sunday."

"Today is Wednesday," Jessie noted. "Other than Kelly Martindale, have you allowed anyone else access to your home while you were gone?"

"No."

"Did you come upstairs when you got home today," she pressed. "Perhaps to change?"

"No. Like I told you earlier, I got home and saw Kelly right away when I got to the stairs. I ran out of the house immediately. This is the first time I've been upstairs since I got back."

So far everything he'd told her comported with the theory that was forming quickly in her head. She pressed on.

"When you left last week, did you go in a rush? Not have time to make the bed or take dishes downstairs?"

"No," he answered, glancing at the unmade bed. "Eileen is very particular. She would never leave an unmade bed or a dirty dish. Everything has to be just so. She's always complaining that our maids don't do as good a job as she does."

"So she wouldn't have left it like that?" Jessie said, pointing at the bed.

"No way."

"Are these yours?" she asked, looking at the clothes folded on the dresser and the sneakers on the floor in front of it.

Carl walked over to get a closer look at the outfit. He reached his hand out.

"Don't touch anything," Ryan reminded him.

Landingham pulled his hand back and instead peered closely at the clothes before kneeling down and studying the sneakers.

"None of this stuff is mine," he finally said.

Jessie tried to contain her excitement.

"Can you look around and tell me if anything is missing?"

Landingham looked at her with skepticism.

"How would I know? We have a lot of stuff."

Jessie tried to stay cool, tried not to raise her voice.

"I don't mean anything valuable, like jewelry or technology. I'm thinking clothes—maybe your favorite T-shirt for lounging around the house, that kind of thing."

Landingham disappeared into the walk-in closet, with an officer in tow.

"What are you thinking?" Ryan asked quietly.

"I have a theory but I want to hold off until I get an answer from him."

It only took another moment for Landingham to call out. He emerged from the closet with a proud expression his face.

"Something *is* missing—my favorite pair of pajamas. I only wear them occasionally but they're super comfortable. They're silk, navy blue. The hanger they were on is on the floor in there."

Jessie sensed Ryan's eyes on her and turned to face him, trying to corral the thoughts pinballing in her head.

"Here's what I think happened," she said slowly. "Lots of people around here leave town for stretches of the summer. That means lots of empty homes. I think this guy, the killer, is a squatter, but not just a regular one. He's a guy who knows the neighborhood well, its rhythms and the people who live here and vacation elsewhere."

"You think he's a local?" Ryan asked.

Jessie nodded, honing her hypothesis with each new word.

"I think he's like Randy out there if Randy didn't have a home base. Maybe he's homeless. Or maybe he fell on hard times or had a run-in with the law. Whatever the reason, this guy has been camping out in people's homes when he knew they'd be gone."

"It would be hard for a homeless guy to know the vacation schedules of residents," Carl offered.

"Good point," she replied. "More likely he's someone who has or had interaction with locals and heard their plans. He could be anything from a barista to a waiter to an employee at a property rental agency. Whoever he is, I don't think he followed Priscilla Barton into the Bloom house as part of some home invasion. I think he was already there because he knew the Blooms were out of town."

No one spoke for a moment as the idea settled in.

"Same at this place," Ryan added, getting on board. "He must have known the Landinghams would be gone too."

"Right. But something went wrong there," Jessie said, turning to Landingham. "Were you supposed to come back today?"

"No. For the last five years, we've left on a Thursday and came back a week later on the Sunday. I..." He stopped mid-sentence.

"What?" Jessie demanded.

His face turned pink as he answered.

"I came back early. I told Eileen I had a business meeting. But it was really so I could spend time with Kelly without worrying about getting caught." He paused before adding a question. "Does this mean she died because of me?"

"So the killer must have thought he had half a week left," Jessie mused, ignoring Landingham's anguished question. "He was likely napping in the bed here after a little snack, enjoying the silk pajamas. Then some girl wakes him up, thinking it's Carl. She runs when she realizes it's not him. He chases her. Maybe in the past he would have just snuck out."

"But she's seen him and he's already on the hook for one murder," Ryan interjected.

"Exactly," Jessie agreed. "He can't let her give a description to the cops, so he pursues her down the hall. Her heel breaks at the stairs. Either she falls or he pushes her. Either way, he finishes her off in the foyer. But before he can go back upstairs and change into his own clothes, Carl here comes home. So he has to bail, barefoot and in silk jammies."

Carl was standing in front of them in horror-stricken silence. But neither Jessie nor Ryan were focused on his feelings of guilt right now.

"So we're not dealing with a thief," Ryan said, more to himself than to her.

"No, not unless you count the stocking, which feels like it's a whole other thing. We're not dealing with home invasions or theft. We're dealing with a guy who wants to live these people's lives, relax in their homes, wear their clothes and eat their food. That's probably what he was doing up until the run-in with Priscilla Barton. And that encounter seemed to set something off in him."

"After her, then Garland and the girl today, it's like he's got a taste for it now," Ryan noted.

The mention of Garland's name felt like a slap across the face. In all the excitement, Jessie had forgotten about her murdered mentor. She suddenly felt like Carl looked: guilt-ridden. But she pushed the feeling away. She was on a roll and she knew that Garland would rather her focus on catching his killer than mourning his loss.

"Yeah," Jessie said, before adding something else that had just occurred to her. "It means something else too."

"What?" Ryan asked.

"There's no way this guy ran out of here in silk pajamas, only to attack you minutes later in that cabana wearing all black, including a ski mask. There just wasn't enough time."

"So what are you saying—that we have a squatter killing people and another guy in the same neighborhood wearing all black and attacking cops in broad daylight?"

"That's exactly what I'm saying," she replied.

Her mind reeled at the thought: two violent offenders operating in the space at the same time but apparently unconnected to each other. She thought she was getting a handle on the squatter killer. But the other attacker confounded her. Who was this mystery man?

Chapter Twenty One

Kyle was still riding a wave of adrenaline when he got back to Claremont.

After changing clothes in Rick's 4Runner, he was now out of that stifling black outfit and wearing a casual T-shirt, shorts, and a baseball cap. He walked into the Claremont Colleges Honnold/Mudd Library and made his way to the restroom in the Finance section. When he was safely in a stall, he texted Rick's burner phone that it was time. While he waited, he made sure that everything was in order. He set the 4Runner key on the toilet paper dispenser and began undressing.

His body ached more than he would have liked. The altercation with Ryan Hernandez hadn't gone as smoothly as he'd hoped. The guy didn't look it in his cheap detective's suit, but Hernandez was shockingly strong. Apparently Jessie liked the big boys. The embarrassing truth was that if Kyle hadn't had the element of surprise and been on top of him in their fight, he wasn't certain it would have gone his way. Next time he'd take proper precautions.

He was almost done when he heard the bathroom door open and Rick whistle the opening bar to *The Bridge on the River Kwai* theme song, the sign that it was him entering. Kyle coughed twice to confirm and Rick stepped into the stall next to him. Neither of them spoke.

Kyle slid his clothes, cap, and the key under the dividing wall between the stalls and waited for Rick to do the same. Less than two minutes later, Kyle flushed the toilet and stepped out of his stall, now wearing the khaki slacks, button-down shirt, and loafers that Rick had on moments earlier.

The keys to his Prius, along with his personal phone, the one he knew was being tracked, were in the slacks pockets, along with his wallet and

ID. He checked himself in the mirror briefly, then left the bathroom and headed in the direction of the parking area where he knew his car would be waiting. As he exited the restroom, he noticed Agent Poulter sitting unobtrusively in an easy chair across the way. He nodded at him and smiled.

He was just reaching the bottom of the main stairwell in the library lobby when Poulter and Agent Cress fell into step behind him. Once they were all outside, Poulter called out to him. Kyle turned around, a broad, phony smile plastered across his face.

"What can I do for you, Agents?" he asked politely.

"You're here at the library for hours on end," Poulter said. "I'm wondering why you're spending you're time in the finance section. I think it'd be better spent in criminal justice, don't you?"

Kyle kept the smile wide, knowing Poulter was just letting off some steam, clearly frustrated at having nothing on him.

"You know, Agent," he said mildly, "other guys who just got freed from prison after a miscarriage of justice might consider this harassment and call their lawyers on the spot, but not me. I know you're just doing your job."

"Our job is to arrest you when you slip up, Voss," Agent Cress growled.

"Slip up?" Kyle repeated innocently. "I don't know what you mean. This is the new me. I'm on the straight and narrow. It's all clean living from here on out. I'm squeaky clean or whatever other cliché you care to use."

"You're not fooling anyone," Poulter said acidly.

Kyle smiled sympathetically, ignoring the blond, muscular guy who walked past the three of them in a T-shirt and shorts.

"I'm not trying to fool anyone, Agent," he said patiently. "I'm just trying to lead my life. Did it ever occur to you that I felt bad about you guys having to sit outside my townhouse in near hundred degree heat? I could have checked out those books and read them at home. But instead I studied them in the cool, air-conditioned library so you two could get a little reprieve. And this is thanks I get, to be accosted and insulted?"

Neither agent had an immediate response to that. Seeing them stand there mutely filled him with glee. He tried to rein in the snark as he continued.

"To make it easier on you guys, here's my plan for the rest of the day. I'm going to stop off at the market, pick up some sushi and maybe some wine if I'm feeling wild. Then I'm going to binge a few episodes of *Mindhunter* and crash early. You can let your night replacements know. In the meantime, I promise to drive slowly."

He didn't wait for a reply. Instead he turned and headed for the parking garage. As he walked, he went over the plan for the night in his head. It was true that he would be having sushi but there would be no wine.

He needed to keep his head clear because he was going out tonight.

Jessie was so anxious that she could barely eat.

They were in a holding pattern right now, unable to take any tangible steps until they heard back from others. They were waiting for any results from the fingerprinting and DNA testing at Carl's place.

They'd convinced the local D.A. to ask a judge to approve a warrant to search all the unoccupied homes on the Strand but the Homeowners Association was fighting it. Apparently they didn't think that the police marching up and down the Strand searching homes was a great look. Meanwhile Jessie was waiting for a call from an eager young MBPD researcher named Jamil Winslow, who was following up on a hunch she had.

In the interim, they'd decided to have a light bite in sight of the Pacific Ocean. They sat on the outside patio at a hipster gastropub, waiting for their food.

"I feel like, even though we're only in our thirties, everyone here is looking at us like we're old-timers," Ryan said, trying to break the tension.

Jessie smiled tightly. She didn't feel chatty but she didn't want to be rude. They both sipped iced tea silently. She tried to give herself a mental break and appreciate the slightly lower temperature that arrived as late afternoon began to bleed into early evening. The break didn't last long.

Ryan got a call just as their food came.

"Bad news," he said when he hung up. "There were no unusual prints found at the Landingham house and DNA results won't be back until tomorrow."

Jessie shook her head in amazement.

"That's stunning if he was squatting there," she said. "It means he's been extremely diligent about wearing gloves and wiping surfaces down."

"He can wipe up prints," Ryan agreed. "But not DNA. Remember, I ordered the killer's clothes and shoes be sent to forensics. Between that and whatever they pull from the bed sheets and stocking, it's not crazy to think we'll have something to go on tomorrow."

Jessie sensed a note of uncertainty ion his voice.

"But …" she prodded.

"*But* if what they find doesn't match someone already in the system, we'll still be stuck."

Jessie took a bite of her turkey wrap and chewed slowly.

"How is it?" Ryan asked.

"Not bad at all," she said, finding the chewing motion unexpectedly relaxing. "But not worth fourteen bucks. What about you?"

"Same. I feel like we're being charged half for the food and half for the view."

"It *is* a nice view," she admitted.

"Mine's better," he said.

It took Jessie a second to figure out that he was talking about her.

"So debonair," she said, batting her eyes elaborately. "You don't look so bad yourself."

Because his original dress shirt was ripped and bloody, he had borrowed an extra T-shirt from one of the officers until they stopped at a local shop and picked up a new work shirt. Jessie had insisted he buy the sea foam green one. Despite his initial protestations, he eventually agreed. She knew he secretly liked how he looked.

"Thanks," he said, blushing slightly.

Jessie had a brief flash of taking the shirt off him again later tonight but pushed it away. The way this case was going, the chances that they'd have any opportunity for intimacy this evening were somewhere between slim and none.

Suddenly she felt a wave of shame at having thought about her own pleasure when Garland had been dead less than twenty-four hours. She knew the old guy wouldn't take offense. In fact, he'd probably be happy that she was allowing herself a few moments unconsumed by grief. But knowing it and believing it were two different things.

"I'm going to call Dolan," she said out of the blue.

Ryan, who was still lingering in their romantic moment, looked confused but nodded. Jessie pretended not to notice and dialed the FBI agent's number. When he picked up, she dived right in.

"Hey Jack," she said. "How's it going? I need an update on Kyle."

"Nice to hear from you, Jessie," he replied laconically. "I'm well. Thanks for asking so sincerely. How are you?"

"I've been better."

"Yes," he said, dropping the sardonic tone. "I heard about Garland. I'm really sorry."

"Thanks, Jack. I appreciate that. To be honest, I'm working a case, the one he was handling when he was killed, and staying focused on it has been good for me. It's been a helpful distraction; keeps me from losing myself, you know?"

"I do. That's what alcohol did for me until a few months ago when I decided to focus on big waves exclusively, if you'll recall."

Jessie did. When she'd first met Jack Dolan while working on an inter-jurisdictional case, he was almost as focused on getting sauced as solving the murder they were investigating. But soon afterward he'd quit drinking entirely. Now he used surfing, always a hobby, as his method of escaping the madness. She could picture him on the other end of the line as they spoke, his silvery hair wet, his skin salty and his face tanned and crinkly from hours in the sun.

"Unfortunately, Jack, I don't balance very well on a surfboard, so I'll have to use work as my mental vacation."

"I just want you to take a moment to process that. You're saying investigating murders is your way to de-stress and navigate grief. Maybe you should let me give you a lesson. I promise we'll start with baby waves."

"A discussion for another time," she told him. "Right now, I need you to tell me where my ex-husband was this afternoon."

"Why? Is everything okay?"

"Actually, Ryan was attacked this afternoon here in Manhattan Beach. At first we thought it was related to the case we're working, but now I'm not so sure."

"Hold on a second," he said, obviously reading something. "I just got the field notes from our day surveillance team. They handed off to the night guys about a half hour ago. It looks like Voss spent the whole day in the Claremont area. He was mostly home in the morning. The he ran some errands in the afternoon, spent several hours reviewing finance textbooks at the college library in the afternoon. He's home having sushi right now."

"How do you know that?" Jessie asked, surprised.

"He told my guys. Despite my repeated requests that they not engage directly with him, they couldn't help themselves. He tends to taunt them with his waves and smiles when he's driving around. Anyway, there was a little chat outside the library, during which he mentioned his dinner plans."

Jessie felt a surge of frustration rise up in her throat and tried to swallow it down before responding.

"I don't know what to do with the fact that your agents sound like they're getting uncomfortably chummy with the man who tried to kill me. But I'll set that aside for now. Where exactly was Kyle from about two p.m. to four p.m.?"

She heard Dolan rustling through his papers. While she waited, she chomped down aggressively on another bite of her wrap.

"It looks like he was at the library that whole time, Jessie," he said apologetically. "My guys say he never left their sight except for occasional short bathroom breaks."

Jessie turned that over in her head, trying to make sense of it. Of course, even if Kyle had an airtight alibi, that didn't mean he hadn't somehow gotten a cartel goon to do his dirty work for him. If that was the case, all this surveillance was probably a waste of time.

"Do they know why he was at the library in the first place?" she asked, grasping at straws.

"He's been there a lot lately, actually," Dolan said. "They think he's trying to bone up on new financial regulations that came down while he was behind bars, so he can ace those job interviews."

"That's weird," Jessie mused.

"What is?"

"In all my years with him—in college, living together after graduation, as a married couple—I never knew him to be much of a studier. He was always more of a 'scrape by' kind of guy."

"Maybe prison really did change him," Dolan suggested teasingly.

"Don't even say that in jest, Jack," she told him. "I will come to your office and beat you down if I have to."

She heard him chuckling at his ability to get a rise out of her.

"I'm just kidding," he said. "Of course it's all an act. But he's convincing some other people, kiddo. You should prepare yourself for him to be surveillance-free by the end of this week."

"Great," Jessie muttered. "Now I've got to add that to the worst to-do list in history: keep your recently discovered sister in good mental health, solve the murder of your mentor, and now, keep an eye out for your murderous ex-husband. What happened to the list with stuff like going to the market and replacing your air filter?"

"Hey, you chose this life," he reminded her.

"Did I though?" she asked.

Before he could answer, she heard a buzz and looked at her phone. It was Jamil, the researcher from MBPD.

"I gotta go, Jack. Let me know if Kyle makes any moves," she said before unceremoniously clicking over to the other line and asking, "What have you got?"

Jamil was clearly excited as he answered.

"Something good, I think."

CHAPTER TWENTY TWO

The woman, whose name was Nancy, kept giving Jessie nasty looks. Her first words upon their arrival were "The MBSHOA offices usually close at six p.m. and it is highly unusual to conduct business outside normal operating hours."

Clearly, she'd lost whatever contest the Manhattan Beach Strand Homeowners Association office staff had held to determine who had to stay late and she was letting Ryan and especially Jessie know it.

Luckily, Jamil Winslow, the polite police researcher from MBPD, had called prior to their arrival and specifically requested that a staffer stay late to walk some LAPD folks through a few documents. Even Nancy knew that refusing a direct request from the police wasn't an advisable option. But that didn't mean she had to be nice about it. So she wasn't.

Her answers were largely monosyllabic and when she was asked for documents, she tossed them over without explanation. Jessie suspected that part of Nancy's animosity was related to the D.A.'s request for the search warrant to access unoccupied homes, which was still pending. Despite being on opposite sides in that dispute, Ryan tried to be cordial with her, but Jessie was losing her patience quickly.

"So this is every person who lost a home or sold one under duress along the Strand in the last year?" she asked through gritted teeth.

"I can't get into people's heads to determine if they were under duress during the time of sale," Nancy said officiously.

Jessie sighed deeply for about the fourth time during their visit. She fought the strong desire to tug on one of the many tight gray curls bouncing tauntingly off the woman's heavily permed head.

Nancy was in her early sixties, with sharp, mean features and cold, light blue eyes. She wore a long floral dress that seemed far too fussy for the summer weather. The foundation on her pinched cheeks was starting to crack slightly after a full day of scowling at people. She was obviously used to being home by now, probably judging the contestants on *Wheel of Fortune* as she sipped rosé in her garden room.

"By duress, I mean folks who sold their homes at well under market value," Jessie said, trying again to be agreeable.

"Those sales are included, as are home losses due to foreclosures, bankruptcy, divorce settlements, and the like. All Strand residents agree to financial transparency in exchange for the privilege of living in such a desirable neighborhood. It's a sacrifice that I'm sure folks from your ... locality are happy not to have to make."

Jessie felt her fists clench into tight little balls, furious with this imperious woman and angry at herself for being baited.

"Do you live on the Strand?" she heard Ryan ask with a tone of studied, insincere civility she had no idea he was capable of.

"I do not," Nancy answered after a painfully long pause. "My home is a few blocks up the hill to the west. I have a better ocean view from that vantage point."

"I'm sure," Ryan agreed, his voice mostly sugar with just a touch of acid. "Let me ask you, if you had to pick the resident who moved out recently who had brought the most disrepute upon the neighborhood, who would that be?"

Nancy only had to think for a second before replying.

"Barnard Hemsley, without question."

"Why him?" Ryan wanted to know.

"Mr. Hemsley is an extremely difficult man," Nancy said.

Jessie made sure to only look at the woman, certain that if she glanced at Ryan, she'd burst out laughing at Nancy describing someone else as difficult.

"Go on," Ryan urged Nancy to continue.

"The man had no respect for the MBSHOA rules and regs. He repeatedly hosed down his deck with chemical cleansers that would drip onto the Strand walking path proper."

"Why is that so bad?" Jessie wanted to know.

Nancy gave her a disdainful look before consenting to answer.

"In part, it was because of the strong bleach-like scent. But more importantly, people walk their dogs on the Strand. They invariably lick any liquid they see. More than one got sick. Owners were irate."

"Anything else?" Ryan wondered.

"Many things," Nancy said primly, handing over the file. "Mr. Hemsley is not married. Instead he chose to have loud parties with young women at all hours. He had no respect for our noise ordinances. He routinely left his deck furniture on the walking path, blocking pedestrian traffic. He put a wooden rocking chair on a section of greenery across from the Strand that only permits approved public seating and landscaping. He tried to have the balcony of his third floor enlarged so that it extended out over the Strand itself. Not only did it violate zoning ordinances, it created a safety hazard. If a chunk of the thing broke off, it might have landed on some baby being pushed in a stroller. There are at least another half dozen violations in the file."

"So what happened?" Jessie asked, morbidly fascinated.

"Well, this went on for several years. Mr. Hemsley is a lawyer and he seemed to enjoy the endless court battles. But the law was on the side of the MBSHOA and he started racking up significant fines, which he refused to pay. That only increased the subsequent fines. Eventually he was over five hundred thousand dollars in arrears. That's when the court told him he had to pay everything at once or have the home seized."

"Did he pay?" Ryan asked, clearly as curious as Jessie.

"Eventually, yes," Nancy said. "But not without strings. He ended up selling his house for well below market value and using some of that money to pay off the fines. It seemed he wanted to intentionally lower the property value. He also made sure to sell the home to people we later learned weren't really Strand types. We would have tried to get them removed as well, if being nouveau riche social climbers wasn't against the bylaws."

Nancy shook her head, appalled at the very thought of the unpleasantness.

"So where is Hemsley now?" Jessie asked.

"He's still in Manhattan Beach. But he's moved slightly inland. Now he lives in Manhattan Township. Have you heard of it?"

Jessie and Ryan shook their heads.

"It's a gated community," she said with just a hint of superiority. "They have their own HOA, thank god. The homes are smaller and more tightly packed together. But they have excellent security. Frankly, I think he moved there just to create havoc for a new set of people."

"Where is this place?" Ryan asked.

"Just off Marine Avenue. It's about a five-minute drive from here. You shouldn't have much trouble finding him."

"Why is that?" Jessie asked.

"I suspect the guards will happily take you to him. I hear everyone there hates him too."

Nancy was right.

The guard at the main gate to Manhattan Township turned up his nose at the mere mention of Barnard Hemsley's name, though he had to fight off a slight smile when he learned the LAPD wanted to question him. He offered to lead them to the man's house and they accepted.

As he drove ahead of them slowly, Jessie took in the homes in the neighborhood. They weren't all that different from the houses one might find in any well-to-do, cookie cutter suburban community. There were only a few real distinctions.

One was that Manhattan Township abutted a major movie studio lot and a nine-hole golf course. They could see multiple soundstages in the distance when they crested the rolling hills and the fairway for the seventh hole when they descended. Another difference was that the entire neighborhood was completely enclosed, only accessible through manned security gates. Once inside, there was no way of guessing that they were in one of the most expensive zip codes in America.

The guard slowed to a crawl as they reached a house at the top of a hill, with a view in every direction. Ryan pulled up next to him.

"Aren't you going to introduce us?" he asked.

"Are you kidding?" the guard said. "I already have to deal with that guy about twice a week. There's no way I'm going to interact with him if I don't have to, not even to see him brought down a peg. Besides, I think your badges will make more of an impression than any introduction from me."

"Any advice?" Jessie asked.

The guard smile wryly.

"If you were a neighbor or delivery person or a new guard, I'd suggest take a Zen approach and say don't let him get under your skin. But you're cops, so I say do your worst. I'd love for him to try to resist you guys and pay the consequences. Good luck."

He drove off, leaving them to deal with the neighbor from hell on their own. They parked on the street in front of his sizable home and walked up the cobblestone path to his front door. The sun was just starting to set and the orange-tinted light reflected off a small lake on the golf course below.

If not for the anxiety of the task at hand, Jessie might have wanted to linger on the moment. Ryan, who was focused exclusively on the task at hand, didn't notice. Before she could mention it, he knocked on the door. While they waited, Jessie thought she heard the distinct sound of Metallica's "Enter Sandman" coming from somewhere inside. She hadn't even met him and the guy was already a cliché.

After about thirty seconds without a response, Ryan rang the doorbell and knocked louder. Jessie was pretty sure that right after that, she heard the song volume go up. She glanced over at Ryan, who nodded to indicate that he'd noticed it too. They waited another thirty seconds, after which Ryan turned to her with that steely, severe gaze she never liked to be on the receiving end of.

"Two can play this game," he growled. He began pounding on the door loudly and relentlessly, and then added, "You want to make sure that doorbell's still working?"

Jessie knew what he wanted and pushed the button once, then again and again, until she lost count. It took another full minute before the door finally unlocked. They heard Barnard Hemsley before they saw him.

"Whose ass do I need to kick tonight?' he shouted as the door swung open.

Chapter Twenty Three

Barnard Hemsley was a mess of a human being.

Though he was only about five foot nine, he had to weigh at least 250 pounds. His thinning, clearly dyed black hair looked shaggy and wild, like it hadn't been brushed in days. He wore cargo shorts and a bright pink, loose-fitting, short-sleeved button-down shirt that was open to his sternum, exposing his grayish, equally wild chest chair. He had on sunglasses despite the lack of sun and the fact that he was indoors. He looked to be in his late-thirties, though his doughy complexion, wrinkles, and blemish-covered skin suggested hard living well beyond his years.

His question about whose ass he needed to kick lingered in the air as he took his visitors in. Even with the sunglasses hiding his reaction, Jessie could tell that he sensed he wasn't in the presence of just another neighbor couple.

"Who are you?" he demanded, his mistrustful voice mixing appropriately with the Metallica lyrics in the background, something about sleeping with one eye open.

"Are you Barnard Hemsley?" Ryan demanded, taking the initiative.

"What's it to you?" Hemsley asked petulantly. The smell of bourbon on his breath was strong.

"I'm a detective with the Los Angeles Police Department. We have a few questions for Mr. Hemsley."

"What if I said he wasn't here?"

Just then, a ghostly pale, painfully skinny brunette wearing bikini bottoms and a half T-shirt with the phrase "my boobs are down here" scrawled across the chest appeared in the hallway behind him.

"Where did you hide the coke, Barney?" she called out before seeing they had guests and unconvincingly adding, "You know I like it better than Pepsi."

Ryan looked at the guy with a mix of annoyance and pity.

"Barney," he said calmly. "This can go smooth or bumpy. It's up to you. Answer our questions honestly and we might be out of your... hair in a few minutes. Make things difficult and it could be a long night for you and your Pepsi-loving companion."

Barney took off his sunglasses and slid them into the breast pocket of his shirt. His brown eyes were bloodshot and he had dark bags under them. For half a second, Jessie thought she saw apprehension in them. Then he seemed to rediscover his inner jerk.

"I won't be pushed around," he said indignantly. "I'm a lawyer, you know."

"Yes," Jessie agreed mildly, speaking to him for the first time. "We did a little research on you, Barney. And despite your copious experience in the divorce space, you might want to rethink how aggressive to be when it comes to criminal law."

"Criminal law? I don't know what the hell you're talking about."

"That's why we'd like to talk to you, Barney," Ryan reminded him.

"We're not friends," Hemsley barked. "You don't get to call me Barney. And I still don't know who you are. You could be some con man posing as a cop for all I know."

Ryan removed his ID from his pocket in a casually unhurried manner before showing it to Hemsley. Jessie knew what he was up to. The hope was that Hemsley would get so riled that he'd do something impulsive— push one of them or make a sudden move—anything that would allow them to take him into custody, or at least threaten him with that to get the upper hand.

"My name is Detective Ryan Hernandez," Ryan said slowly. "I'm with Homicide Special Section, a unit based out of downtown's Central Station."

Jessie saw Hemsley's eyes widen briefly at the word "homicide" before he regained control of himself. He looked over at her.

"And who's the skirt?' he demanded derisively.

"The skirt?" Jessie repeated, laughing in his face as she pulled out her own ID. "What is this, 1947? The skirt is Jessie Hunt, criminal profiler based out of the same station. Now are you going to be responsive, Barney?"

She made sure to punch the name emphatically and saw that it had the desired effect. Hemsley's face turned redder than his eyes and his breathing got puffy.

"I don't think so," he said wheezily. "Unless you have a warrant, you have no right to be here. And I'm not coming out. So you can go back downtown and question some of those street bums in your neck of the woods. I'm done with you."

He started to slam the door but Ryan stuck his foot out before it could close, stopping it.

"That's not going to work for me, Barney," he said, popping hard on the "B" in his name. "You see, I heard what your gal pal in there said and I couldn't help but notice white powder around her nostrils. So we've got plain view evidence supporting our suspicion that there is illegal drug activity going on in this house. We also have reason to be concerned that if we waited for a warrant, you would try to dispose of that evidence. We can't allow that to happen."

"You're making that up," Hemsley protested. "You didn't see anything on Brandee's nose."

Ryan looked at Jessie, shaking his head in disappointment.

"That's exactly what someone hiding large quantities of cocaine in his house would say," he noted. "I'm afraid that's not going to fly, Barney. So I'm going to give you one more chance. Come out here and answer our questions. It's entirely possible that your honest responses could send us on our way. Or you can continue to be difficult and have the worst night of your life, at least until you try to comb that rat's nest on your head."

The line was so over the top that Jessie was sure Hemsley would sense that Ryan didn't actually want him to suddenly become cooperative. He had to see that this detective was itching for him to do something, baiting him into a bad decision. But Barney seemed unaware. And since he was quite likely both drunk and high right now, she was pretty confident that he'd oblige. She was right.

"I pay your salary," Hemsley shouted angrily. "You have no right to talk to me that way. I ought to put you in your place!"

"Are you threatening me, Barney?" Ryan asked, taking a half step forward and dangerously shrinking the empty space between the two men. "It sounds like you are. What would you do, sit on me?"

That was all Hemsley could take. He shoved his finger in Ryan's chest, poking him angrily as he opened his mouth to retort. But before he could get a word out, Ryan had grabbed the guy by the finger, twisted his arm back behind him, and kicked out the back of his left leg so that he collapsed to his knees. Within seconds, Hemsley was in cuffs and Ryan was reading him his rights.

"By the way, Barney," he said when he finished. "You don't pay my salary. But you did help pay for the station where we're taking you. So it should be a real nice cell."

Hemsley tried to spit on him but he was short of breath and the saliva didn't go far enough, instead merely dribbling down his chin before getting hopelessly entangled in his abundant chest hair.

"Can you go collect the lady of the house?" Ryan asked Jessie. "I have a feeling she might be more receptive to us than Grumpy here."

Jessie nodded and headed down the hall, pretending not to hear the names Barney called her as she walked away, nor the loud grunt of discomfort from him that followed. When she rounded the corner into the living room, she found Brandee passed out on the couch. She shook her gently to wake her up, then helped her to her feet and put a pair of cuffs on her.

"Hey," Brandee protested hazily. "I thought we weren't using those until later tonight, Barney."

Jessie wasn't sure how to respond.

At least I still have the capacity to be surprised.

"We're starting the party early," she finally said.

"Party!" Brandee shouted in response, her voice managing to drown out even Metallica.

Chapter Twenty Four

Barney lawyered up right away.

Ryan and Jessie had expected it. But since there was no way he was going to talk back at his place, bringing him into the station was a risk worth taking. While they waited for his attorney to show up, they hung out in the MBPD lounge, which was infinitely nicer than their own.

The one downside was that the holding room where they were keeping Brandee was just across the hall and her constant shrieking was giving Jessie a headache.

"I was going to wait until Brandee sobered up," she said to Ryan. "But maybe if we question her now, we can at least get her to stop screaming. What do you think?"

"I'm willing to try anything," he said.

Jessie bought a frosted cupcake and they walked across the hall, where Brandee seemed to be trying to destroy her vocal cords in just one night. Jessie held up the dessert in front of the woman and the screeching stopped immediately.

"This is yours if you answer a few questions for us," Jessie told her.

Brandee stared unblinkingly at the cupcake and swallowed hard.

"Barney told me I should never answer any cop questions until he gave me permission."

Jessie pulled out a chair and sat down, putting the cupcake between them on the table.

"A couple of things on that," she said. "First, I'm not a cop. I'm a profiler, so you're good on that front. Second, Barney may be in a lot of trouble and I'm not sure it's in your best interest to be following his instructions right about now. And maybe most important of all, I can't give you the cupcake if you don't talk."

Brandee licked her lips. Her internal struggle lasted about two more seconds.

"What do you want to know?" she asked.

Jessie saw Ryan, who was standing behind Brandee, smile and stifle a laugh with a cough.

"Where was Barney this afternoon?"

"Work, I assume," Brandee replied.

"Where's work?" Jessie asked.

"Down on Highland, just off Thirteenth Street. His office is right across from Cousin Willy's Waffle Hut."

"When did he get home?"

"I don't know. I was out at the nail salon until six. He was there when I got back."

"What about yesterday evening? Do you remember where he was between eight thirty and ten p.m.?"

"Last night?" she said, straining to recall the details. "Oh yeah, I went out with some girlfriends for dinner and drinks. I left around seven. He was still at work. I got home after midnight and he was asleep on the couch with the TV on. I woke him up and we went to bed."

"What about Monday, late afternoon to early evening?"

"Oh, come on. That was so long ago. How am I supposed to remember?"

"Try, Brandee," Jessie pushed. "It's important."

The woman scrunched up her face. It looked like the effort of remembering was physically painful.

"I know we ordered takeout for dinner that night—Thai food. I don't remember the time but it was dark when I opened the door to get it so it had to be pretty late. But before that, I don't know. Most days he works until six or seven. I assume he did the same on Monday. Can I have the cupcake now?"

"Yes," Jessie told her, passing it over.

Brandee immediately began scarfing it down. While she ate, Jessie and Ryan stepped into the hall.

"We ought to be able to verify his location using his phone," Jessie said.

"Yeah," Ryan conceded. "But his office is within walking distance of both crime scenes. He could have left the phone at work intentionally while he committed the crimes."

"Possible," Jessie agreed. "But the attack on Priscilla felt like a crime of passion. I wouldn't think he'd leave his phone back at the office if this happened on the spur of the moment."

"Maybe the killing itself wasn't part of the plan but sneaking into someone's house was? Maybe he wanted to spy on her as part of some other personal fetish he had. Then he might try to hide any digital evidence that he was there."

Jessie wasn't as convinced. But something Ryan said reminded her of one of Garland's notes.

"Hey," she said suddenly. "Based on what Brandee said to me, Barney is into handcuffs. Let's ask her if he has any other fetishes."

Ryan's eyes lit up as he got what she was hinting at. They returned to the room, where Brandee was licking the remaining cupcake crumbs off her lips.

"Does Barney like pantyhose, Brandee?" Jessie asked without warning.

"Huh?"

"Pantyhose, stockings—does he like to wear them, or use them during kinky sex games?"

Brandee's expression changed quickly from confused to delighted.

"Not that I know of," she said with a devilish smile. "But I'd be open to it. I have enough pairs."

"You do?" Jessie asked. "Why is that?"

"I like this one kind, their shop is based here in Manhattan Beach. They're super popular, or at least they were for a while. I used to always try to make Barney buy me a pair whenever we walked by there. I have to have at least half a dozen. Only the best for the best, right?"

"Sure," Jessie replied uncertainly.

Before they could continue, her phone rang. It was Hannah.

"I've got to take this," she said, stepping outside.

"Can I get another cupcake?" Brandee asked as Jessie moved down the hall. Ryan would have to deal with that request.

"How's it going?" she asked when she was outside and out of anyone's earshot.

"It's getting late and I hadn't heard anything from you," Hannah said. "So I wanted to check in."

"I'm sorry. Ryan and I are working this case in Manhattan Beach. It's all mixed up with Garland's death. I guess I lost track of time. Are you okay? Do you think you can handle dinner on your own tonight?"

"Sure," Hannah said, sounding less peeved than expected. "Do you have any leads on the case?"

Jessie felt a pang of guilt for having assumed that Hannah would be focused only on herself. She was clearly still thinking about Garland.

"We do have leads," Jessie said. "But I'm not sure how great they are. I'll let you know if we nail someone though."

"Is there going to be a funeral?" Hannah asked.

Jessie was embarrassed to admit she had no idea. Garland, widowed young and without children, had never talked about family. She wasn't sure who would organize the event.

"I assume so," she finally said. "I'll have to check around. Do you want to go if there is one?"

"I might," Hannah said quietly.

"Let me look into it," Jessie said. "How was your day?"

"Okay, all things considered," she answered, though Jessie could hear hesitation in her voice.

"What's wrong?"

Hannah paused and Jessie could sense her debating whether to come clean. She finally did.

"I don't want to make a big deal of this. But all day I've felt like someone was watching me. I'll look back, but I never see anyone suspicious. It could just be that I'm on edge. But considering everything that's been happening lately, and with your ex-husband getting out of prison, I didn't want to totally dismiss it. You said he's been systematically trying to destroy your life. And I guess I'm part of your life. So I thought I should mention it."

Jessie was the last person to disregard generalized suspicions about being shadowed and she considered Hannah more than justified in her concerns.

"I'm glad you told me," she said. "I'm going to have a team of officers sent over there right now to do a welfare check. I might even have a few of them stick around until we get back. Okay?"

"Yeah," Hannah agreed. The fact that she didn't complain about Jessie overreacting or having a bunch of cops in her personal space was the strongest proof that he sister was truly worried.

"Text me when they get there and give you an all clear, all right?"

"I will," Hannah promised, "as long as you keep me updated on Garland's case."

"It's a deal," Jessie said.

After hanging up, she immediately called Captain Decker and requested a security detail for her place. He didn't need much convincing.

"I'll have a unit over there in fifteen minutes," he assured her.

"Thanks, Captain," she said, relieved that she didn't need to work to convince him.

"Not a problem. How's it going down there?"

As she was about to answer, Jamil Winslow, who was frowning in concentration, hurried past her on the way to the room where Ryan and Brandee were.

"Lots of leads but nothing definitive yet," she admitted. "We just got word a second ago that a local judge is going to approve a warrant to have unoccupied homes on the Strand searched. But he's not letting us start until tomorrow at eight a.m. I guess he's trying to find a compromise, but it doesn't help us much. I'm worried about another attack tonight."

"I can try to lean on him," Decker offered. "But sometimes that backfires with judges in these independent jurisdictions."

"That's okay," Jessie said. "I don't want to risk him pulling the warrant altogether. Besides, we're about to take another run at a suspect soon. His lawyer is on his way. We're hoping we can still get him to talk."

"Do you like him?"

"He doesn't have a good alibi for any of the attacks. And he's definitely a shady character. But is he a killer? Too soon to tell."

"Well, keep me posted."

"Yes sir," she said and almost ended the call. But a thought made her stay on the line. "Captain, are there any plans for Garland Moses's funeral? Is anyone planning anything?"

"I am," he said, sounding surprised that she didn't know. "He has a niece back east who's coming out but they weren't close. She asked me to handle things. There will be a service on Friday. He was Jewish and his faith prefers it happen sooner than that. But there's been a massive outpouring from all over the country. At least fifty FBI agents plan to attend, several hundred LAPD folks as well. Even some families of victims are flying in to honor the man who gave them some measure of peace. We wanted to give them all time to make it. I assumed you'd want to be there."

"Yes sir."

"We'll make sure to save you a seat. In the meantime focus on this case. But don't forget to take care of yourself. You're my top profiler now. I can't afford to have you out of commission."

"No sir," she said before realizing he'd already hung up.

No pressure there.

Chapter Twenty Five

The second Jessie stepped back into the station, she could sense that the energy of the place had changed.

Glancing through the window of the interrogation room, she saw that Barnard Hemsley's attorney had arrived. Ryan was in the break area, having an animated conversation with Jamil Winslow, the police researcher they'd been working with all day.

For someone so young and inexperienced, Jessie had been impressed with him. He was only twenty-four and Manhattan Beach wasn't exactly a criminal hotspot, so her expectations for the junior staffer assigned to them were low. But Jamil, short and skinny, was sharp, relentless, and seemingly indefatigable. Even at this late hour, he showed no sign of slowing up. He was also ambitious, having already asked if there were any openings at Central Station. She promised she'd look into it.

"What's up?" she asked when she joined them.

Both men looked up at her. She could tell from their excited expressions that something had happened.

"Why don't you tell her?" Ryan suggested.

The younger man nodded and dived right in.

"Lots of updates for you," he said breathlessly. "First, the GPS on Hemsley's phone shows him at his office at the time of all three murders, as well as the attack on Detective Hernandez. Of course, that proves little based on the theory that he could have left it there while committing the crimes."

"Okay," Jessie said. "That helps a little. We certainly can't eliminate him based on that."

"Right," Jamil agreed. "But more interestingly, he had connections to both female victims. Detective Hernandez showed photos of both female victims to Brandee. She didn't know Priscilla Barton. But she did recognize Kelly Martindale. She said that she and Hemsley would sometimes see Kelly out at clubs in the area with 'an old dude' that Barney knows.

"Barney and Carl are friends?"

"No," Jamil corrected, "at least not according to Brandee. In fact, she said that Hemsley considers Carl an arrogant jerk. But they definitely know each other from when Hemsley lived on the Strand."

"Okay, that's something we can work with," Jessie said.

"There's more," Jamil said. "Guess who owns the house Barnard Hemsley used to live in, before he sold it at a loss?"

"I couldn't possibly."

"Garth and Priscilla Barton! He sold them the place about a year ago."

Jessie looked over at Ryan, who was smiling.

"What are the chances that these are all coincidences?" he mused.

"It's a small community," Jessie countered. "And knowing these people doesn't mean he had a motive for killing them."

"No," Ryan conceded. "But it's more than we had before. And if this is some kind of obsessive stalker fetish thing, we now have proof that he was at least aware of both these women. Plus, according to what Brandee told us, he has easy access to that brand of stockings. Tell her the other thing, Jamil."

"Oh, right," Jamil said excitedly. "Based on court records, at least three of Hemsley's recent clients have homes within a block of either the Bloom or Landingham residences."

Ryan picked up from there.

"So it stands to reason that he might have met with those clients at home, within peeping distance of the houses where these attacks took place."

Jessie considered the information.

"All of that is supposition," she pointed out unconvincingly. "None of it is definitive."

"No," Ryan conceded. "But nothing we're finding makes him seem *less* guilty."

Jessie nodded. She couldn't argue with anything he'd said, though something still made her reluctant to jump on the Barney train.

"Let's go talk to him and his lawyer," she offered. "Maybe he'll be chattier if confronted with all this. Thanks, Jamil."

The young researcher smiled enthusiastically. Jessie suspected this was the biggest case he'd ever dealt with and he was riding the adrenaline high.

When they stepped into the interrogation room, Barney was seated, while his lawyer remained standing. The man was the same height as his client but perhaps a hundred pounds lighter and ten years older. He was bald, save for a narrow strip of gray along the back of his head. He had a mild manner which was reinforced by the sweater vest and Dockers he wore.

"Giles Orlean," he said, extending his hand to both of them. "I represent Mr. Hemsley. It's an honor to have such celebrated law enforcement personnel in our sleepy little town."

"Not so sleepy of late, Counselor," Ryan pointed out.

"And not so celebrated either," Barney piped up. "Giles here told me about your reputation, Jessie. I didn't realize you were the chick who was under fire for going on racist Facebook rants. Maybe that explains my unprovoked, violent arrest. Trying to overcompensate by bringing down a rich white guy, huh?"

Jessie held her tongue, fully aware that Barney was trying to bait her in front of his lawyer.

"Barnard," Orlean said soothingly, "we might all be better served by lowering the temperature a bit. I'm quite confident that we can clear up this misunderstanding with a little open communication."

"I wholeheartedly agree," Ryan said, dropping photos of Priscilla Barton and Kelly Martindale on the table in front of them. "You're currently under arrest for assaulting a law enforcement officer. Depending on the information we get from you now, those charges could change to include multiple counts of murder. So maybe you'd like to help yourself."

"Who are these women?" Orlean asked, unfazed by the sight of two dead bodies.

"I was hoping Mr. Hemsley could help us out with that," Ryan said, pointedly not calling him Barney this time.

"I don't recommend that Mr. Hemsley respond until you give us a little more to go on, Detective," Orlean replied.

Before Ryan could counter, Barney started talking.

"Hey, I recognize that one," he said, pointing at Kelly Martindale. "She's the hottie that asshole Carl Landingham was nailing when his wife was out of town. I remember she and Brandee grinding on each other at a dance club a few months ago. It was pretty awesome, though Carl didn't seem to love it. She's dead now? What a waste."

Jessie saw Giles Orlean roll his eyes in frustration.

"What about the other woman?" Ryan asked.

Barney squinted as he leaned in to get a better look.

"I don't know that one," he said. "She's not bad, although she looks like she's getting a little long in the tooth."

"She was thirty-one. And you *do* understand that you're talking about a dead woman, right?" Jessie reminded him. "You don't seem to have an ounce of compassion about that."

"Why should I care?" Barney demanded. "I don't know her."

"Are you sure about that, Barney?" Ryan asked, dropping the formality. "Because you sold your house to her last year."

"What?" Hemsley replied, less annoyed by Ryan's first name dig than he'd been earlier. "I sold my house to some oil and gas goober from Louisiana, name of Barber or something. He would have paid twice my asking price but I wanted to screw the Homeowners Association by lowering the property value. Plus, he was a real wannabe. I figured he'd annoy all the snooty locals real good."

"That 'wannabe' was Garth Barton and this is his wife, Priscilla," Ryan told him.

"Okay," Barney said after looking again. "I never met her, only the husband. I'm sure she was just as annoying as him."

"Did you find her annoying when you passed by her place and the Bloom house to see your nearby client?" Ryan asked. "Did you tell Kelly Martindale she was a hottie when you visited the two clients you had less than a block from Carl Landingham's place?"

"I don't know what you're talking about, man," Barney insisted, though he seemed less forceful than he had been earlier. "I meet my clients at the office, not their homes."

"Always, Mr. Hemsley?" Jessie pressed. "Do you want to lock yourself into that statement? Because we can check your phone data against the dates of these meetings and if they don't match up, you could be in some real trouble."

"Ms. Hunt," Giles Orlean said, sounding huffy. "I think we've had just about enough of these scurrilous allegations."

"Mr. Hemsley," Jessie said flatly, ignoring Orlean, "both those women were murdered within walking distance of your office, as was an LAPD profiler. You had multiple clients in the immediate vicinity of the murder scenes. You have personal connections to both female victims and no firm alibi for any of the times of death. You can see why this is a problem, can't you?"

Barney Hemsley looked at her as if he didn't have a care in the world.

"Maybe for you. But not for me. I didn't kill anyone and I'm getting my legal assistance pro bono, so this is just an evening's entertainment, as far as I'm concerned."

Ryan and Jessie looked at Orlean, confused. Red-faced, he explained.

"Barnard represented me in my divorce," he said sheepishly. "He did it gratis …"

"Because his wife was such a bitch," Barney interjected.

"And I said that if he ever got into a criminal scrape," Orlean concluded, "I would do the same for him."

"Well then," Ryan said, "it's lucky there are no formal charges yet, Barney, because this could get really expensive otherwise. We haven't even gotten to the pantyhose."

"What pantyhose?" Barney demanded.

"The ones found around both female victims' throats, the same brand that Brandee says you bought multiple pairs of for her."

"Whatever, man," Barney said dismissively, though a hint of uneasiness had crept into his voice. "I don't pay attention to pantyhose brands. She wanted them. I bought them. Pretty cheap way to keep her happy and compliant, if you ask me. And what about the profiler, did he get 'hosed' to death too?"

He chuckled at his own joke. Jessie had a flash of Garland lying on the ground, old and weak, his body broken and his brilliant mind forever gone. Her stomach turned over even as her heart started beating double time. She leaned in close so that their noses were almost touching and growled at him.

"That profiler was my friend, you sick bastard. And if you're responsible for his death, I'm going to make sure you burn for it."

Hemsley laughed.

Jessie suddenly felt her blood rush faster. Her cheeks flushed and for the briefest of seconds, her vision got cloudy. She felt a blind fury come over her and made no attempt to fight it.

She was just raising her arm to clutch the man's throat when she felt Ryan's arms wrap around her chest, physically lifting her up and carrying her back several feet. She struggled to shake free but his grip was unbreakable. Orlean stood in front of his client, trying to reduce the tension by eliminating her sightline to him.

"I understand you're upset, Ms. Hunt," he said. "But that kind of outburst isn't productive for anyone."

"Typical emotional woman," Barney jeered. "Getting your panties all in a bunch, or should I say pantyhose? I don't give a rat's ass about your profiler buddy. What do you think of that?"

"Shut up!" Orlean hissed at him as Ryan dragged Jessie out of the room and slammed the door.

"I'm gonna kill him, Ryan," she snarled.

"If we're lucky the state will do it for us," he told her. "But not if you mess it up. Go take a walk. Cool off. I'll handle this, okay?"

"Aren't you pissed?"

"Of course I am. I want to rip his trachea out, just like you were about to. But I want justice for Garland and those women more. So I have to swallow my anger. But rest assured, if this guy did it, he's not going to be laughing much longer."

After several deep breaths, Jessie nodded. She knew he was right. Going off on Barney Hemsley, whether he was guilty or innocent, wouldn't do anything to help Garland.

"I'm going down to the pier," she said.

"Good idea," he agreed. "I'll check in with you in a bit."

He gave her a kiss and squeezed her arm affectionately. She tried to force a smile but found she couldn't. As she walked toward the station exit, he returned to the interrogation room.

"Barnard Hemsley," she heard him say loudly, "I'm placing you under arrest for the murders of…"

The door slammed shut, cutting off the rest of the sentence. She knew what came next. But it didn't make her feel any better.

CHAPTER TWENTY SIX

The wind had a surprising bite to it.

As hot as the day had been, with the sun now having set, the ocean breeze felt suddenly malevolent, slicing against her sensitive skin with unexpected ferocity. She embraced it.

There was something clarifying about the sting. It cleared her mind and forced her to focus. The fury of the interrogation room was already starting to fade, replaced by a desire to put the pieces together, to ensure that Barney Hemsley paid the price for his actions.

She felt a buzz in her pocket and checked her phone. The text was from Hannah, saying the cops had arrived, cleared the building's lobby and parking structure, and were currently doing a sweep of both the condo and the whole thirteenth floor. Jessie texted back thanks for the update and asked her to relay any additional ones.

She returned the phone to her pocket and took several additional deep breaths, trying to clear her head. She was at the very end of the pier, in the same spot where she'd stood with Ryan earlier today, seemingly a lifetime ago.

In the distance she could see the lights of several massive cargo ships, all waiting to unload their freight at the Port of Los Angeles. Much closer in, she saw a few surfers braving the black waters, oblivious to the sea monsters she felt sure were lurking just out of sight. Monsters liked the dark, though not necessarily the one she was hunting.

While Garland had been killed at night, both Priscilla and Kelly were murdered when the sun was still out. That was a brazen act, especially in such a highly populated, heavily trafficked area. It seemed hard to believe someone could have done those things and simply left the scene without being noticed. And Barney Hemsley, with his flyaway hair, rotund stomach, and garrulous nature, didn't strike her as the type to recede into the shadows unnoticed.

Frankly, despite the mounting evidence against him, Barney didn't seem right for this in any number of ways. The guy had everything—a huge house, a lucrative career, and a pliant, adventurous girlfriend.

More compellingly, he just didn't seem like an obsessive, furtive guy. All his desires were right out in the open. If he was into choking attractive women for kicks, Brandee seemed amenable. And had she not been, he surely could have found women willing to play that game for the right price. Plus, he just didn't seem like the squatter "type," whatever that meant.

Yes, he had clear connections to both women. But they weren't as personal as Ryan had suggested. And they could have just been coincidences. Barney was a grotesque human being. But he was also smart, or at least wily enough to almost taunt her into assaulting him. The idea that he would kill women that he knew could be traced back to him, even if they were crimes of passion, seemed doubtful.

Jessie couldn't dismiss him as a suspect. But for the time being, she decided to set him aside. In fact, it might be worthwhile to do something unusual. Instead of trying to get into the killer's head, maybe she should shake things up and get into someone else's head: Garland's.

Something had made him come back to this neighborhood and return to that house on his own, late at night. That was not standard procedure. What was eating at him so much that he couldn't wait until the next day to check it out? She pulled out his notepad and flipped through it to the last page.

"OTB," "missing h," and "fetish?"

Those were the only words scribbled on it. The last two phrases made some sense. She was confident that "h" referred to hose, though she wasn't sure what "missing" meant. "Fetish?" was clearly a reference to liking to choke women with stockings.

The top result when she'd searched the term "OTB" online was for off-track betting, which seemed random and unlikely. But he wouldn't have written it down if it wasn't important. She pulled out her phone and searched the term again. She got the same results. Frustrated, she was about to put the phone away when it occurred to her that since he considered all three terms to be connected, perhaps she should put in all three terms together.

Shy typed "OTB" again and had just started to add "missing h" when she realized she could now change "h" to "hose." She stopped mid-type as her brain did the equivalent of a silent, internal fireworks show. It was all suddenly clear, as if someone had laid out the facts, buffet-style, in front of her. She recalled Brandee's comment earlier, "only the best for the best, right?" Only the Best wasn't just a description of the stockings. It was their name: OTB.

She cleared the search screen and started fresh, this time typing in the phrase "Only the Best stockings pantyhose." The first result was for the boutique that Brandee was so fond of, right here in Manhattan Beach, less than a quarter mile from where Jessie now stood. She tapped the link. The page loaded to reveal the company's website, complete with its logo, a diamond with the letters "OTB" inside.

Before she knew what was happening, she found herself running. Doing her best to ignore her tender back, she moved as fast as she could, until she was back in front of the Bloom house where both Garland and Priscilla Barton had died.

Since the second death, the department had assigned an officer to stand watch at the home 24/7. She flashed her ID at him and hurried past, going inside and taking the stairs two at a time. When she got to the master bedroom, she turned on the light and hurried over to Gail Bloom's dresser. After putting on gloves, she slowly opened the top drawer and looked in.

Just as she had remembered, the drawer was messy, as if it had been rifled through. But if her hunch was correct, it wasn't the killer who'd gone through Gail Bloom's underwear but Garland himself, just before he'd been killed. She looked through it now, just as he had, and made the same suspicious discovery that he had: Bloom had no OTB stockings.

Jessie again unknowingly did the same thing Garland had and knelt down to see if perhaps one had fallen under the dresser. But there was nothing there. She closed her eyes and thought the scenario through. In the end, she came to the same conclusion that her mentor had.

The logical assumption would have been that the killer was in the house, maybe even this bedroom, when heard Priscilla Barton enter and grabbed a stocking to use as a weapon. But if that was the case, then one would assume he'd leave the other stocking here in the bedroom or that it would have been found during the search of the house later. But it hadn't.

Furthermore, not only did Gail Bloom have no pairs of OTB stockings in that drawer, she didn't seem to own any pantyhose at all. If that was true then there was only one other conclusion to draw—the killer had brought the stocking *with him* into the home and had it in his possession at the time of the attack.

What kind of man sneaks into a wealthy stranger's home to squat, and when discovered, kills the woman with a high-end stocking that he had already had in his possession? And what kind of man uses that same brand of stocking to kill a second woman two days later?

While the obvious answer was a very troubled man, the other, perhaps less obvious but equally intriguing one, was this: a man for whom OTB stockings held some personal significance.

Jessie closed the drawer and walked back out of the bedroom, down the stairs, out of the house, and back to the MBPD station to do the same thing Garland would have done if he hadn't been killed: research hosiery.

CHAPTER TWENTY SEVEN

A half hour later, Jessie stared the computer screen, ignoring the exhaustion that made her eyes periodically droop.

She didn't know what she expected, maybe a news story saying some guy obsessed with these stockings had been arrested for stealing them or accosting women wearing them. But there was nothing like that.

In fact, her initial research suggested that the company was both beloved and well-respected. The testimonial page was littered with effusive praise from customers. Review sites like Yelp were equally enthusiastic. Jessie couldn't find a bad word about the quality of the product or the customer service, either online or in the boutique just four blocks over from where she now sat.

Ryan and Jamil sat at nearby computers and she could tell from their silence that they were meeting with the same level of frustration. Ryan in particular looked annoyed. When she had returned to the police station earlier, she saw that any satisfaction he'd gotten from arresting Barney had quickly faded. It was clear that, based on the evidence they currently had, they'd be lucky if he ultimately faced trial on the assault charge for poking Ryan in the chest, much less murder.

She stood up and stretched. Glancing out into the station bullpen, she saw Sergeant Breem. He was the man who'd initially refused to let her go upstairs last night after Garland's body was discovered. She later learned he'd also honchoed the crime scene for Priscilla Barton's murder. Breem was in civilian clothes and looked to be leaving for the evening. On a whim, she stepped outside and chased after him as he headed out the door.

"Sergeant Breem," she called out, "can I bother you for a second?"

Breem turned around. He looked tired but when he saw it was the profiler whose mentor had been murdered the night before, he made a gallant attempt to hide it.

"Of course," he said, "and I'm off duty so call me Drake."

"Drake," she said after catching her breath. "How long have you worked for the department?"

He thought about it for a second.

"About fifteen years. I grew up here back when it wasn't so hoity-toity. But I couldn't get on the force here for a while so I went to work for the Long Beach PD. But I live in the area, surf right down the block from here most mornings, so when a position opened up back here, I jumped on it. I've been here ever since."

"So you know the community pretty well?" she asked.

"I think I can safely say that," he said, smiling.

"What do you know about Only the Best?"

"The boutique?" he said. "It's over on Manhattan Avenue, just off the main drag."

"No, the company more generally," she said. "As you may know, both female victims were strangled using that brand of stocking, which made me think the killer might have some animosity to the brand or the store. But I've been looking online and I can't find a whiff of controversy related to it. I thought maybe a well-steeped local might know something that didn't get out to the general public."

"Wow," he said. "Nothing immediately comes to mind. I know they had an executive shake-up a few months ago. But that seems kind of dry compared to what you're looking for. I don't recall there ever having been a criminal incident. Sorry I can't offer more help."

Though deflated, Jessie smiled.

"That's okay. It's my fault for thinking there might be some secret key that unlocked this whole thing. There almost never is. You should go home and get some rest. I don't want you too sleepy to catch those waves tomorrow."

Breem smiled, apparently whisked away by the very idea.

"All right. By the way, I'm really sorry about Mr. Moses. I know you two were close. I actually followed his career. He was a real genius. I was a bit of a fan boy. I'm planning to go to his funeral on Friday if I can get the time off. Will I see you there?"

"Almost definitely," she said.

As he headed off, she felt her phone buzz and checked it. Hannah had texted.

Cops didn't find anything suspicious. One is staying outside our apartment. Another is downstairs in the lobby with the guards. The other one left.

Jessie texted back:

Thanks for the update. Still working the case. Running out of leads for the night but don't wait up just in case. Tell the cops we'll relieve them when we get back.

Hannah texted her back with a thumbs-up emoji and she walked back inside to rejoin Ryan and Jamil, who looked even more downtrodden than when she'd left.

"Why don't you head home, Jamil?' she suggested. "You've done so much for us today and you look like you're about to collapse on your keyboard."

"That's okay," he said. "I have tomorrow off so I don't mind. This is more interesting than anything I've worked on so far this year. I kind of don't want it to end."

"Sick puppy," Ryan said, chuckling slightly. It was the first time Jessie had seen him smile since she'd returned to the station.

"We're all a little messed up to keep trying to get blood from this stone," she said. "But I was going to try just a little longer, if you guys don't mind."

"What do you have in mind?" Jamil asked.

"I was just talking to Sergeant Breem and he mentioned that there was a change of leadership at the company a few months back. He didn't seem to think it was all that noteworthy. But sometimes there are skeletons in seemingly boring closets. Maybe we do a little spring cleaning?"

"That sounds stunningly tedious," Ryan said forlornly. "I'm definitely going to need a coffee break before diving in. What about you, kid?"

Jamil nodded and the two of them went to the break room, leaving Jessie alone with her pitiless screen. She sighed deeply, blinked a few times, and then dived back in.

First she went to the "news" tab of the company website and searched through the press releases. As she scrolled through, she noticed something odd. In the last four months there were only three of them, all related to sales figures and upcoming product rollouts. And in the period from about six months ago going back five years, there were a total of eleven releases, all of a similar nature, with occasional updates on promotions and expansion.

But from January 17 through February 2 of this year, there were thirty-one press releases on everything from online sales in Argentina to a new air-conditioning system in the company's Torrance production facility. No topic was too small to earn a news item. At no other time but during this two-week window did such minute changes or updates get such exhaustive discussion.

It's almost like the public relations team was trying to flood the site with inconsequential information in order to hide some real news they hoped might get missed.

All of a sudden, Jessie felt a renewed sense of energy. She started printing out all the releases from that period. By the time Ryan and Jamil returned, she'd placed ten releases on each of their desks, along with highlighters.

"What's all this?' Ryan asked dourly.

"Welcome back, boys," she announced happily. "We're about to do a deep dive."

"Into what?" Jamil asked with more enthusiasm than Ryan had expressed.

"I'm not sure yet. But this company is desperately trying to hide something and we're going to find out what."

CHAPTER TWENTY EIGHT

I t was Jamil who found it.

Jessie had given them a few more instructions before they started: they were looking for a press release that included actual news, not just puffery. It would probably be bad news hidden among positive updates and made to look like it was just business as usual. It was likely personnel related, referencing a promotion, lateral move, retirement, or resignation. The press release Jamil identified had almost all of that.

"It's dated January twenty-second and titled 'New Design Addition Expected to Spur Growth in International Markets,'" he began. "The release runs three pages, the bulk of which touts the latest hire in the Creative Design team, Massimo Torini, formerly of the Italian women's wear company, Max Ultra."

Jamil skimmed the page before continuing.

"There's a long description of his accomplishments, as well those of two other designers he's bringing with him. It mentions several additional promotions and department shifts, foremost among them the promotion of Greg Petrie to head of the design unit. Lastly, it notes that the now-former Head of Design Pierce Cunningham will move to an advisory role. The rest of the press release mentions several adjustments to the marketing and finance teams, none of which seem to be more than title alterations without actual changes in job description."

Jessie smiled broadly.

"Why did you pick that one, Jamil?" she asked expectantly.

"Well, it sure looks like they were trying to hide one piece of bad news in a long announcement about good news."

"I bet Pierce Cunningham would agree with you," Jessie said.

Ryan, who had been poring over a document of his own, poked his head up with an energy that Jessie knew meant something big.

"If you think he was bummed about that news, he must have really hated this."

"What?" Jessie asked excitedly.

"It's from January twenty-eighth. So we're talking just six days after he got dumped as head of the design unit. The title of the release is about as dry as they get—'Torrance Facility Upgrades Increase Productivity.' They go on for a page and a half about things like a nicer break room and revised production line standards. Then there's this one: 'Design Advisor Pierce Cunningham has chosen to take advantage of the company's early retirement program.' After that, the announcement goes on for another paragraph about the solar panels in the parking lot."

"That's it?" Jessie asked. "No 'we thank him for his service' or 'OTB wishes him success in his future endeavors'?"

"Nothing like that," Ryan replied.

Jessie did a quick term search through all the press releases and found that other than those two references, Pierce Cunningham's name, which was mentioned repeatedly prior to January 17, never came up again.

"Gentlemen," she said, after relaying that information, "does it seem possible that almost all thirty-one of these press releases were specifically designed to hide one piece of information— that OTB fired Pierce Cunningham quickly and unceremoniously and didn't want anyone to notice?"

Both men nodded in agreement. Jessie continued.

"I think it's time we get to know Mr. Cunningham a little better, don't you?"

After another half hour, they had a pretty good picture of the man. His biography was impressive, if pretty straightforward. He grew up in rural West Virginia, where he excelled as a student and got a scholarship to the University of Virginia. Success there led to acceptance at the Parsons School of Design, where he got a graduate degree in Fashion Studies. From there, he worked at several New York fashion houses until moving west to become the head designer for Joben Couture.

Nothing overtly suspicious so far.

Somewhere in that stretch, he met Irina Letsch, an up-and-coming runway model, who would subsequently become his wife. A few years later, he co-launched Only the Best, a lingerie company, where he was responsible for multiple designs.

In several profile pieces, he was described as having a reputation for being "eccentric" and "mildly obsessive," with a "strong workaholic streak," but nothing else was shockingly out of the ordinary. He and Irina moved into a huge house on the Strand and had been there ever since, which meant for well over a decade.

Seems like a man who would know when his neighbors were in town or away on vacation.

Everything appeared fairly conventional. He was forty-eight. He and Irina, nine years his junior, had no children. Photos of Cunningham showed him to be a pleasantly bland-looking man, slightly paunchy, with blond hair that was just starting to recede.

For a fashion marvel, he's not particularly memorable to look at, the kind of guy who could move around largely unnoticed.

While Jessie reviewed his biography, Ryan was checking the legal databases and hit, if not gold, at least, bronze.

"Cunningham was involved in a legal proceeding on January fourteenth," he said. "It concerned a financial settlement with an undisclosed individual for an undisclosed amount. He is not specifically named, but his LLC, PC Perspectives, is. Cunningham is the only person affiliated with the company. The settlement language is extremely vague, with only a passing reference to restitution for emotional injury."

"That's interesting," Jessie mused.

"There's more," Ryan added. "I find his name associated with a complaint that was filed on January ninth and withdrawn on the tenth. The complainant was an anonymous female and the specifics of the complaint are unknown. Since it was withdrawn, all of that information was expunged from the system."

Jamil waved his hand enthusiastically.

"I think I might have an idea about the nature of the complaint."

"Do tell," Jessie said.

"I've been going through the social media accounts of OTB employees from the beginning of the year, trying to see if I could get their unofficial take on Cunningham. There was nothing, which I found more suspicious than if there was some bad-mouthing. So I accessed some web archive sites to see if there were any deleted tweets or posts of interest."

"How did you do that?" Jessie asked.

"There are several sites that archive tweets, posts, and Instagram stories. A few take periodic screenshots. It gets a little complicated and I can give you a primer later. But here's the point. I found one I think you'll be interested in. It's from a design associate at OTB named Annie Cole, dated ten twenty-one a.m. on January first."

Ryan and Jessie came over to screen and looked at the tweet. It read:

Can't believe what happened last nite. Boss cornered me at New Year's Party at The Portico. Hit on me. When I said no, tried pull my skirt down. Scary stuff. #meto.

"She misspelled 'me too,'" Ryan noted.

"Amazingly, that may be the only reason we don't already know about this," Jamil replied. "If she'd typed the hashtag correctly, it would have joined all the others in that trending topic and there's no way it would have stayed hidden. Multiple people would have taken screenshots and done research. Considering that she mentions The Portico, where they held the party, it would have been traced back to Cunningham within hours. But because she deleted it less than fifteen minutes after posting it on New Year's Day morning, it slipped under the radar. Unless you knew to specifically look for something like this, there's no way you'd ever find it."

"Okay," Jessie said, her mind working faster than she could get the words out, "so she deleted the tweet. But I think we can safely assume that wasn't the end of it. Clearly sometime between January first and January ninth she made the decision to file a complaint against Cunningham. And it would appear that she was convinced to withdraw the complaint by the end of business the next day, which suggests some furious legal wrangling during that time, leading to the settlement agreement on January fourteenth."

"Right," Ryan agreed, following her logic. "And once the settlement was agreed to, surely including requirements of confidentiality, the company was free to start the process of quietly jettisoning Cunningham."

Jamil jumped in.

"Interestingly, on January fifteenth, the day after the settlement was finalized, Annie Cole posted an Instagram story saying she was leaving OTB and moving back to her hometown of Kansas City to start her own boutique. That timing can't be coincidental."

"Nope," Jessie agreed. "And neither was the timing of OTB's plan to flood their website with press releases and slip in the notification about Cunningham's changed status. OTB is a publicly traded company. They're required to disclose details like management changes. So they mention a revised role for him, and then six days later make a passing reference to him retiring early. No one even notices."

"Someone noticed," Ryan said, looking at his own computer screen.

"Who?" Jamil asked.

"Cunningham. After he 'retired,' he had a real run of bad luck. He transferred all his stock options to an unknown individual. I'm guessing that might have been part of the settlement with Annie Cole. Irina divorced him and got the house. He had to move into an apartment in Westchester, which he was subsequently evicted from. He even had his car impounded. He was also briefly institutionalized, involuntarily, for self-harm. It seems that a few months after he moved out Irina found him in their bathtub. He'd taken a bunch of pills. He spent time at the hospital physically recovering before being transferred to a longer-term care facility. He was only released a couple of weeks ago."

"Where is he now?" Jessie asked.

"No idea," Ryan said. "He dropped off the radar after leaving the hospital."

"Maybe we should check in with Irina to see if she's seen him or can give some insight into where he might hide out," Jessie suggested, pulling up her contact information and calling her cell phone.

"Straight to voicemail," she said, frustrated.

They all sat at their desks silently for a moment.

"Wait, I have an idea," Jamil said suddenly, picking up his own phone.

"I kind of like this kid," Ryan muttered to Jessie, who nodded in agreement.

"Hi, Nancy," Jamil said, pausing briefly for a reply before continuing, "Yes, I'm sorry, I know it's late. But you were so helpful with those folks from LAPD before that I was hoping to impose on you again."

Another pause as the voice of Nancy from the MBSHOA could be heard on the other end of the line.

"Yes, ma'am," he said. "I was wondering if you could provide me with the emergency number for Irina Cunningham. She's not answering her cell phone and I know all Strand residents are required to keep an emergency beacon on their person in case the HOA needs to quickly disseminate information to the community."

After another pause, this one longer than the last, he thanked her and hung up.

"Well?" Ryan demanded.

"Nancy said she'd happily contact Mrs. Cunningham but that it wouldn't do much good right now as Irina is currently on a red-eye flight to Paris, where she'll be vacationing for the next few weeks. Apparently they go every year at this time and Irina decided not to cancel and let a little divorce ruin her summer. So we'll have to wait a few hours to get hold of her."

"No we won't," Jessie said excitedly as she stood up.

"Why not?" Jamil asked.

"Irina left today for a weeks' long vacation, a vacation Pierce knew was happening. Her house, the house he used to live in, is empty. I think we can guess where he might be squatting tonight. What's his address?"

CHAPTER TWENTY NINE

Pierce Cunningham knew he should leave.

He'd been sloppy with the second woman. Even though he was always careful to wipe down his prints when he stayed somewhere, he was sure that he'd made some mistake in his mad dash from Carl Landingham's place.

Even if the cops didn't nail him with DNA or something, they eventually would because of the stocking. Of course, he used one for the first murder of the nosy neighbor because he had it on him. He always carried the memento of his time as the celebrated designer of a beloved garment.

It just so happened that it was in his hand at the exact time the neighbor discovered him hiding in the corner of the living room. If he'd had a glass vase at his disposal, he might have used that after he chased her into the foyer. At least that's what he told himself. But there was a poetic justice to taking a life with something he'd created. Birth, death, rebirth—something like that.

Using the stocking for the second murder had just been a crazy coincidence. The girl who fell down the stairs happened to be wearing them. Using it as a weapon of death had worked out well for him once before. It only made sense to use it again. Part of him thought it was meant to be. It couldn't have just been an accident of luck that she was wearing the same brand of hose that had snuffed out the nosy neighbor's life, the same brand that he designed with his own blood and sweat. It was a sign and he couldn't ignore it.

All the same, those beautiful coincidences were sure to blow back on him when someone eventually figured out that the man who designed the stockings used to kill two women had been institutionalized not long after an incident involving violence toward another attractive young woman. He had little confidence that the details of the settlement he'd reached with that whiny bitch, Annie Cole, would stay secret forever. Even if it was in the interest of the jackals at OTB who'd forced him out to keep things quiet, tongues always wagged eventually.

But he couldn't bring himself to leave. After all this was *his* house. Technically it now belonged exclusively to his cold shrew of an ex-wife, who'd had gotten it in the divorce after basically threatening to publicly reveal his drunken moment of poor judgment on New Year's Eve and ruin what was left of his reputation.

But he had originally found the place. He had supervised the renovations that turned it from merely a large, two-story Spanish-style house into a full-on Mediterranean mansion with a third floor, a rooftop pool, and views that, on clear winter days, included snow-capped Mount Baldy over sixty miles to the northeast.

He wandered from room to room, aware that every minute he stayed here put him at risk. Still, he couldn't help but let the memories wash over him: the first night he and Irina had slept here, the rainy morning when she'd told him she had no interest in children. He recalled the first time he'd slept here with someone other than Irina, not long after discovering the credit card statement, the one she thought he didn't know about. It showed she'd spent a weekend at a Malibu bed & breakfast, not alone, when he was working in New York.

He remembered coming back here the first time after having spent a month at the Hazelden Treatment Center in Minnesota, where they tried to help him get a handle on his OCD, his proclivity to self-medicate, and what they politely referred to as his "impulse control issues." He remembered one night when Irina was visiting her mother, sneaking back here with an OTB intern who had been more receptive to his overtures than Annie Cole was. All the memories faded in and out, sometimes twisting into each other.

He suspected the haziness might have something to do with vodka he'd been consuming almost nonstop since crawling through the window with the faulty latch once it got dark outside. Whatever the reason, he found himself in his former bedroom, rummaging through Irina's clothes, the ones she kept in the walk-in closet he'd had built for her, which was bigger than his first apartment in Manhattan.

He tossed dress-adorned hangers onto the floor, trying to keep track of how many of her outfits he'd designed. He opened her dresser drawer, the one that held all the OTB stockings. There were dozens—some sheer, some in colors—all created by him. Even now, though she despised him, Irina couldn't get rid of these.

She loved them too much. Just as so many other women did. Stockings weren't especially popular in Southern California these days. But his creation still held cachet, even if he no longer did. He'd never met a woman who'd worn them who had a critical word to say. They were his gift to the world. He wondered if that would be taken into consideration when he was finally held to account for his sins. The thought made him laugh out loud.

Your honor, my client may have strangled the life out of two innocent women. But he knew how to make a gorgeous pair of hose, don't you think?

He laughed again, even louder this time.

Officer Carrie Shaw was ready to go home.

She didn't have that much longer until her shift ended at midnight and she could feel her concentration fading in and out as she walked the length of the Manhattan Beach section of the Strand, keeping an eye out for anything out of the ordinary.

It had been an unordinary week in town and it was still only Wednesday. Already, three murders had been committed along this very stretch of homes, one a resident, one the mistress of a resident, and one a celebrated LAPD criminal profiler.

Carrie would have liked to have been involved in any of those investigations. But as the newest member of the department, she wasn't even considered experienced enough to stand guard outside the homes that were now crime scenes. She suspected that it was her physical bearing as much as her inexperience which put her at a disadvantage. Though she was athletic and wiry, a former gymnast, she was also petite, five foot two and 110 pounds soaking wet—not exactly an intimidating presence.

So instead of guarding a crime scene or going out on calls, she was stuck walking up and down the two-mile stretch of walking path that constituted the Manhattan Beach Strand. She estimated that in the last three hours, she walked close to eight miles. She didn't even get to take advantage of the magnificent view of the Santa Monica Bay. By the time she took over Strand Patrol from the officer one rung up above her on the seniority ladder, it was already too dark to see the ocean.

Besides, she was supposed to be looking in the other direction, at the houses of people richer than she could ever dream of being. Sometimes she felt like a bit of pervert, peeking into people's homes, spying on private, personal moments, looking for any behavior that might seem suspect.

Just then, and seemingly in a direct rebuke to her, a woman in the house she was passing scowled down at her and dropped her blinds emphatically. Carrie shook her head with a mix of shame and annoyance.

I'm just trying to do my job, lady.

She knew she wouldn't get any dirty looks from the next house. According to her call sheet, the homeowner was out of town for at least the next two weeks.

That must be nice.

She was about to move on when she noticed a light on in a room on the third floor, casting a dull spotlight onto the section of the walking path just ahead of her. That wasn't terribly unusual. Lots of residents set lighting timers when they were out of town to fool potential thieves into thinking someone was home. She started to look ahead to the next house when something that she did consider unusual caught her eye.

The first floor facing the ocean was enclosed entirely in glass. Some of it was comprised of floor to ceiling panes. Other sections were populated by multiple, smaller windows. One of those windows, in the farthest corner of the deck, mostly hidden behind a lounge chair, appeared to be open.

She walked over to get a better look. Sure enough, it was open, if only slightly. She also noticed what looked like fresh footprints on the damp wood deck flooring just outside the window. She pulled out her flashlight and shined it on the panel of window glass, where she was greeted by several handprints.

She took a step back and got out her radio. Considering recent events, it seemed wiser to call it in and be accused of overreacting rather than assume it was the work of a forgetful resident and end up missing the chance to apprehend a potential killer.

She lifted the radio to her mouth and was about to start talking when she heard it. The sound was hard to identify definitively. It was somewhere between a screech and ... a laugh? She couldn't decide whether she was hearing someone cackling in pleasure or shrieking in pain. Either way, somebody was in a home that was supposed to be unoccupied.

"This is Officer Shaw on Strand Patrol. I'm hearing potential sounds of distress coming from the residence of Irina Cunningham, between Second and Third streets. My call sheet indicates she is out of town, but there's an open window on the first floor and a light on the third floor. I'm going in. Send backup."

She turned down her radio so as not to alert the potential intruder and scrambled through the window. Once inside, she unholstered her gun and headed for the stairs that led to the third floor, following the sound of those nearly inhuman squeals. She was halfway between the first and second floors when she lost her footing and landed hard, with a thud that echoed through the house.

Pierce stopped laughing.

He needed to catch his breath. But seconds later, he felt the start of another giggle fit coming on at the notion of being the first defendant ever to use the "I'm a fashion genius" defense against a double murder charge. That's when he heard the loud thumping noise, like someone had dropped a big bag of fertilizer down the stairs.

He fell silent and waited for any other sound. The ones that followed—two consecutive creaking noises—got him moving. After years of living in this house, he knew that two stairs going from the first to the second floor were notorious for their loud groans. He and Irina had learned to step on the outer edges of those stairs to avoid them. But a stranger to the home would have no idea. And that was clearly what he was dealing with.

He turned off the closet light, hurried across the master bedroom, and flicked off the switch for that light too. Then he peeked out in the hall and, seeing no one, prepared to dash into the guest bedroom across the way. But just before he did, an idea sprang into his head. He turned the bedroom light back on and left the door half open, then moved across the hall to the guest room.

About ten seconds later he heard another familiar groan, which indicated that his unwelcome visitor had reached the top of the third floor stairs, where he was. He was positive the person wasn't Irina, who, after years of living here, managed to avoid every creaky spot instinctively.

He heard the soft footsteps of someone who was clearly trying to tip-toe on the carpeted floor. The sound he expected—the squeak as the master bedroom door was pushed open— should be coming soon. Then he'd have to make his choice. Would he hurry along the hall to the stairs and try to escape the house before others, likely an army of police, arrived? Or would he go the other way, toward the intruder?

Just then, the master bedroom door's hinges howled in protest as the door was opened. Pierce opened his own door. Without even thinking about it, he made his choice.

CHAPTER THIRTY

Jessie and Ryan were already in his car and halfway to the Cunningham residence when the call came in.

They'd considered going on foot, but the house was at the southern end of the Strand, almost half a mile away from the station. Besides, their bullet-proof vests were in the car. They were tearing down Manhattan Avenue, just crossing over 9th Street, when Carrie Shaw's radio call came in.

Jessie looked over at Ryan and could tell that they were thinking the same thing. Part of her wanted to warn Shaw to hold off on entering alone. But if someone was screaming in distress in the home, every second might be the difference between saving a life and losing one.

Ryan pulled the car over at the corner of Ocean Drive and 3rd Place, the closest that vehicles could get to the Strand on that block, where they both hopped out. Jessie ignored the sting in her back as she pushed herself out of the seat. They strapped on their vests as they ran to the address.

"Should we try to enter through the window she mentioned?" Jessie asked.

"No time to look for it," Ryan said. "We just have to get in there."

They arrived at a side door and he kicked it, hoping it would fly open. It didn't budge.

"Backup plan," Ryan said, pulling out his gun and taking aim at the knob.

He fired, sending a deafening echo throughout the quiet neighborhood. Then he kicked again. This time the door offered no resistance. He led the way in, gun in one hand, flashlight in the other. Jessie followed close behind, assuming the same posture.

"Shaw said the light was on the third floor," Jessie reminded Ryan, even as he made his way to the stairs.

They moved up quickly, trying to stay quiet enough to pick up the sound of voices or a physical struggle. To Jessie's dismay, they heard nothing. Occasionally they stepped on a creaky step and hoped it wasn't audible upstairs. When they got to the third floor, they inadvertently made even more noise when they reached the top of the landing. Their weight made the floor below them groan softly. They looked down both ends of the hallway but didn't find any lights on.

"You want to go left?" Ryan whispered. "I'll check out the rooms on the right."

Jessie nodded and began moving down the hall. The fact that Officer Shaw was nowhere to be seen or heard was deeply unsettling. She tried to force that concern from her head and just focus on the path in front of her.

She flashed her light into the first bedroom she came to but saw nothing out of order. She was just approaching a second open door when she heard what she thought was a grunt from the last darkened room at the end of the hall. She turned back to alert Ryan by waving her flashlight. But his head was turned away as he stepped into a bedroom, disappearing from sight.

She thought of going after him but a second grunt told her there wasn't time. Instead, she moved toward the sound as quietly as she could. When she reached the open door, she took a deep breath and slid into the room, shining her flashlight.

Lying on the ground, conscious but clearly in bad shape, was a young woman in a police uniform who Jessie assumed was Officer Shaw. Jessie moved the light around the room, looking for anyone else, but found no one. She moved deliberately over to Shaw, who was looking up at her and seemed to be saying something in a raspy, nearly unintelligible voice.

"Bind doe."

Jessie kept moving, even as she tried to process the woman's words. She was almost to her when she figured it out.

Bind doe. Behind door.

She spun around just as the shadow of someone appeared on the wall, swinging something downward toward her. Jessie managed to get her arms up over her head, blocking the worst of the blow as what appeared to be a golf club came crashing down.

Unfortunately, the club did manage to come down forcefully on her right forearm, knocking the gun from her hand. The figure swung at her again. This time she jumped back, avoiding it. But she didn't avoid Officer Shaw, who was right behind her. Stumbling over her, she fell backward onto the floor.

Jessie scrambled to her feet, anticipating another swing of the club. In the distance, she heard Ryan calling out to her. The man, who she could now more clearly identify as Pierce Cunningham, paused on his upswing and dashed over to the bedroom door, which he locked. Then he turned back around, an expression of twisted rage on his face.

"End of the hall!" Jessie shouted as loud as she could. Her words seemed to jumpstart Cunningham, who ran toward her.

She didn't hesitate, stepping over Officer Shaw and rushing to meet him. He was just raising the club again when she lifted her small flashlight and shined it in his face. It had at least part of the desired effect as he squinted and turned his head away. But he didn't stop moving. Before Jessie could dodge him, they collided hard.

Cunningham was shorter than Jessie but had at least fifty pounds on her and she got the worst of the impact. They both toppled over, Jessie backward again, this time with Cunningham on top of her. Shaw was somewhere in the mix as well.

A searing pain cut through Jessie as her raw back landed heavily on the hardwood floor. Through her watery eyes, she saw that Cunningham had apparently lost golf club in the fall. But that didn't stop him from wrapping his hands around her throat and squeezing.

At first she was so stunned, she didn't even process the fact that she couldn't breathe. But a half-second later, the reality of the situation kicked in. Without making the conscious choice, she swung the small flashlight, still in her left hand, upward.

It connected with Cunningham's right temple but didn't seem to do much damage. Her left hand was her non-dominant one and weaker than her right. Still she swung again. This time Cunningham was ready and blocked the blow with his raised right elbow. The light flew out of her hand into the corner of the room.

The only positive was that when he'd lifted his arm to protect himself, Cunningham's grip on her neck loosened slightly, allowing her to get a gasp of air before he crushed down again. Ignoring her throbbing back, Jessie fixed her blurry vision on Cunningham's doughy, enraged face and concentrated. Then, with all the strength she could muster, she swung both of her now balled-up fists toward his head, simultaneously smashing them into his ears.

He howled in pain, again loosening his grip briefly. Jessie used the respite to thrust her head up hard and fast and felt the top of her skull connect with something hard on his face. When she fell back, she saw that blood was already starting to drip from his nose.

Despite his screechy bawling, Cunningham stared down at her with furious intensity and swung his fist toward her face. Jessie closed her eyes in anticipation of the contact. None came.

She opened her eyes again to find that Officer Carrie Shaw had managed to crawl onto her knees and grab his fist with both her hands. Cunningham was frantically trying to yank it free while shoving at the cop with his other hand.

Though her torso was still pinned down by his weight, there was no longer anything constricting her throat. Jessie took another quick breath and swung her fists up again, this time pummeling Cunningham with repeated punches to the nose and eyes. He flailed at her with the arm Officer Shaw wasn't clutching but couldn't stop the barrage of strikes she rained up on his face.

A moment later she heard a deafening crunch and looked over to see Ryan smash through the door like a blitzing linebacker. He rolled to his feet, took stock of the situation, and aimed his weapon at Pierce Cunningham.

Everyone tangled up on the floor froze.

"Wait!" Jessie shouted. "He's unarmed!"

There was another moment of unmoving silence from the three people on the ground.

"In that case," Ryan said as he marched toward them. Without breaking stride, he lifted his right leg and kicked Cunningham, still atop Jessie, sending him careening across the room. The man slammed into the far wall and collapsed into a heap. Ryan moved quickly toward him, pinned his arms behind his back, and cuffed him.

"Can I borrow your cuffs?" he asked of Officer Shaw.

She tossed them to him and he used them to attach the man to a bedpost.

"I think she broke my nose," Cunningham wailed.

"Are you two okay?" Ryan asked, ignoring him.

Shaw nodded. Jessie did the same as she rolled gingerly onto her stomach and slowly got to her feet. Ryan grabbed her arm to steady her. She smiled to let him know there was no permanent damage before turning to Shaw.

"Thanks for the assist," she said with a raspy voice.

"Thank *you*," Shaw replied, her voice equally strained. "He caught me by surprise. If you hadn't shown up, I'd be … thank you."

She grew quiet at the realization of what almost happened to her. The sound of sirens fast approaching filled the air.

"Better call it in," Jessie advised, hoping to help the young cop snap out of her own head and avoid the kind of emotional spiral she knew all too well. "We don't want to get accidentally shot when we've got the guy in custody."

While Shaw did that, Ryan leaned in close and whispered to her.

"How are you really doing? You look like you want to scream louder than Cunningham is."

"Let's just say I may allow myself an extra pain pill tonight, but not just yet. I need to stay clear-headed when we question this guy. I want to be the one to get him to confess to killing Garland. I owe him that."

She wanted to say more but suddenly the full weight of what had just happened—the sprint up the stairs, the feel of her back slamming into the floor, the ache in her throat—all hit her at once.

"Can you help me to the bathroom?" she asked quietly. "I think I'm going to throw up."

CHAPTER THIRTY ONE

Everything throbbed.

Jessie was still in serious discomfort, but the nausea had passed. As she sat in the MBPD interrogation room, listening to Ryan read Pierce Cunningham his Miranda rights, she felt a renewed sense of purpose and strength. She couldn't bring Garland Moses back. But she could at least nail his killer so that he might have some measure of peace when he was laid to rest in less than two days.

She sat quietly as Cunningham agreed to waive his right to counsel and began answering Ryan's questions about the murders. He was forthright, sounding alternately defeated and proud as he relived the particulars of the attacks on both Priscilla Barton and Kelly Martindale. No question went unanswered. No detail was too small to share.

When Ryan was satisfied that he had what he needed, he nodded at Jessie. She delicately got to her feet and leaned over the table between her and the suspect, staring at him silently. His broken nose was bandaged but some blood was still seeping through it. He already had dark shadows developing under his eyes, which were red from where Jessie had punched him repeatedly. Ryan had assured him that they'd take him to the hospital to get checked out once he had answered all questions to their satisfaction. It didn't seem to occur to the man to press the issue.

"Despite the intimacy of our earlier interaction," she began, "we haven't been properly introduced, Mr. Cunningham. My name is Jessie Hunt. I'm a criminal profiler for the LAPD. Do you know what that means?"

"Serial killers and stuff," Cunningham said, expressing inappropriate pride in his answer.

"That's right, at least partly. My job is to get into the minds of criminals to try to understand why they do what they do in order to better determine how to stop them. And I think I'm pretty good at it. But you know who was better?"

Cunningham shook his head, clearly perplexed as to where this was heading.

"Garland Moses," she said evenly.

"Who's that?" he asked disinterestedly.

Jessie promised herself that she would not lose it, as she had with Hemsley. She had to stay cool, for Garland's sake.

"That's the man you murdered on Tuesday night, Pierce," she said, switching to his first name.

"What?"

"Surely you remember the elderly man you strangled with a belt barely twenty-four hours ago, Pierce," she said, surprised at how composed she sounded. "My question for you isn't how, though. We know that. My question is why? I can't figure it out. Was it just bad timing or does your choking fetish extend to old Jewish men with bifocals and worn-out slacks?"

Cunningham looked at her, bewildered, before turning to Ryan.

"Is this some kind of joke?" he asked. "Is she trying to mess with my head?"

"It's not a joke," Ryan said calmly. "Answer her question."

Cunningham looked back at Jessie, still apparently befuddled.

"I don't know what you're talking about, lady. I didn't kill any old man."

Jessie stood up straight, partly to give her back a break and partly to keep herself from leaping at the guy. The control she'd felt earlier was starting to slip away. When she felt calm enough to continue, she replied in a soft, cold voice.

"You just gave us every bit of minutiae on the other murders. Why hold back now? Unburden yourself, Pierce, You'll feel better."

"Listen," Cunningham said, leaning in himself now. "I don't have any problem getting into the details, obviously. If I had killed this guy you're talking about, I'd admit to it. But I've only killed two people in my life. Trust me. I thought I was going to increase the total tonight. You might remember that."

He smiled nastily as he added that last bit. But Jessie was no longer focused on his tone. As her mind raced, she felt a familiar, creeping dread rise in her chest. She leaned back in, boring holes in Cunningham's eyes.

"To be clear," she said, adopting a composed tone she didn't feel inside, "you're saying that you did not kill Garland Moses."

He stared right back with unblinking eyes.

"To be clear," he replied, "I wish I had. This guy obviously meant a lot to you. And I'd love to know that I had ripped him away from you. Nothing would fill me with greater pleasure. But sadly, it wasn't me."

Jessie looked over at Ryan with an urgency he immediately recognized. They hurried out of the room, leaving Cunningham in the care of Officer Shaw, who looked like she wouldn't mind a few minutes alone with the guy.

"What is it?" Ryan asked when they were safely alone.

"I believe him," Jessie told him. "And if he didn't kill Garland, that almost certainly means the person who did wasn't there by chance. It means someone followed him there, stalked him, hunted him. The killer used Priscilla Barton's murder as a cover to kill Garland, knowing everyone would assume they were committed by the same person."

"You can't know that for sure," Ryan protested. "It was a murder scene. Maybe some curious local snuck in to check it out and panicked when Garland walked in on him."

"Maybe, but I don't think so. Don't forget that just this afternoon, you were attacked and almost killed right after we found Kelly Martindale's body."

"Believe me, I remember, Jessie."

"Okay. We know that couldn't have been Cunningham. He fled the scene in pajamas and there was no way he could have changed into black clothes and a ski mask in the intervening time. Besides, you said your attacker was stronger than you. Cunningham clearly isn't."

She saw Ryan started to connect the dots of the picture she was drawing.

"What's your point?" he asked.

"I think the same person who used Priscilla Barton's murder as cover to kill Garland tried to do the same thing with you. I think he was following you and took advantage of the chaos in the aftermath of the Martindale murder to go after you. I think he did these things so that I wouldn't catch on to the pattern."

Ryan clearly knew the answer but asked anyway.

"What pattern?"

"The pattern of going after the people closest to me. This has Kyle's fingerprints all over it."

"But didn't Dolan say his people never lost sight of Kyle? There's no way he could be in a Claremont library studying finance *and* here trying to kill me."

"Dolan's people missed something. I don't know how but they did. Kyle's been planning this for two years. I'm sure he anticipated having an FBI tail. Even if it wasn't him on Tuesday night or this afternoon, that doesn't mean he didn't mastermind the thing, get one of the cartel heavies to kill Garland and come after you."

Ryan didn't argue with her. She could tell that he was coming around.

"Then let's go get him," he said. "Call Dolan and get his address in Claremont."

Jessie was about to do exactly that when she suddenly gasped as the real truth of the situation hit her.

"What?" Ryan demanded, concerned.

"He's not in Claremont. He's been going after the people closest to me. He killed Garland. He tried to kill you. There's only one person left."

She was already running to the car as Ryan muttered the name to himself.

"Hannah."

CHAPTER THIRTY TWO

"I'm telling you, I'm fine."

Hannah repeated it for the third time, trying to keep from sounding annoyed at her big sister.

"Put Officer Nettles on again," Jessie demanded.

Hannah rolled her eyes as she handed the phone to him.

"Jessie," Nettles said calmly, "Beatty and I have been here all night. No one has entered the condo. We just did another search of the building and the floor. We have another car out front and they haven't seen anything unusual either."

Hannah could hear her sister's raised voice through the phone.

"You guys will stay put until we get back, right? We're only fifteen minutes away."

"I promise we're not going anywhere," Nettles assured her.

"Kyle Voss is smart," Jessie barked loudly. "Don't let your guard down."

"We won't."

Jessie hung up and Nettles gave Hannah back her phone, smiling sympathetically.

"She can be a little intense at times," he said.

"That's an understatement," she agreed. "But she's just trying to keep me safe. And from what I've heard, her ex-husband is a stone cold psycho. So I'm inclined to cut her some slack."

"She's usually spot on," Nettles said, "so me too. This isn't the first time we've been at this building protecting her from a killer. She doesn't tend to cry wolf. In any case, Beatty will be downstairs and I'll be right outside if you need me, okay?"

"Thanks."

"And remember the confirmation code," he added. "Don't answer the door unless you get two knocks, a pause, and then two more knocks. Ask who it is, even if you see me or Beatty through the peephole. If I don't answer 'not the pizza guy,' you don't open up. Got it?"

"You've told me this three times, Officer Nettles."

"I'm just being thorough," he replied. "I don't want your sister to kick my ass."

Once he'd stepped outside, Hannah sat on the couch and allowed herself a moment to breathe. She closed her eyes and tried to think of something pleasant, like leaves falling gently from a tree in a cool forest. But it was no good. Her eyes popped back open.

Even though Nettles and Beatty had done multiple searches, as had the other officer before them, she still felt skittish. She resigned herself to the fact that she wouldn't get a wink of sleep until Jessie and Ryan returned. Considering that was supposed to be in less than fifteen minutes, she turned on the TV and fixed her attention on whether Sophia was going to tease Blanche for telling another anecdote about one of her sexual conquests.

They parked right in front of the building.

Jessie ran inside while Ryan reconfirmed with the unit across the street that they'd seen nothing unusual all night. By the time he got to the lobby, Jessie and Officer Beatty were already at the elevator waiting to go up.

They found Officer Nettles right where he said he'd be, just outside the condo door. He gave the official knock and code phrase and Hannah opened the door to let them all in. Jessie could tell that despite her pretense of nonchalance, her sister was relieved to see them.

"Thanks so much, guys," Jessie said to the officers once they got settled. "We've got it from here. Y'all can head out for the night."

Nettles, the grizzled, graying senior officer, and Beatty, the fresh-faced youngster with curly blond hair who joined the LAPD the same month that Jessie started consulting for it, exchanged glances.

"That's okay," Nettles said. "Jimmy and I talked about it and we're going to stick around if that's okay with you. We'll send the other unit home but one of us will stay in the car and the other in the lobby. We can be up here in two minutes if you call."

"That's not neces..." Jessie began before Ryan cut her off.

"Thanks, guys," he said, giving her a disapproving glare. "We really appreciate it. Make sure to keep the receipts for any snacks you get. They're on me."

They nodded and headed out. Once they left, Jessie looked at Ryan quizzically.

"Don't you think they deserve a break after being here all night?" she asked him.

"Jessie, those guys have been off the clock since seven p.m. Tom Nettles and Jim Beatty volunteered for this duty because they care about you. Remember, they were both here guarding this place when your life was at risk. If they say they want to stick around, just say thank you."

Jessie nodded, chastened, and moved to lock the front door and checked that the windows were closed and locked too. Then she turned on the security system. When all that was done, she finally sat down next to Hannah.

"How are you?" she asked.

"Oh, you know, I've been better."

"I hear you. Sorry we were out for so long."

"That's okay," Hannah replied. "Did you get the guy?"

"Kind of. We caught the guy who killed the two women. But I don't think he was responsible for Garland's death."

Hannah didn't look shocked.

"You think that was your ex-husband?"

"I do," Jessie confirmed. "I also think he tried to kill Ryan this afternoon. That's why we were in such a rush to get back. You seemed to be the next logical choice."

"Why?" Hannah asked.

"Because he's going after the people I love," Jessie said, as if the reason was as clear as day. There was a long pause during which both of them processed the words that had just been said.

"Oh," Hannah finally replied, clearly at a loss for a moment. When she regrouped, she changed the subject. "But can't you just have him arrested?"

"We can't prove it's him yet," Ryan explained. "In fact, we haven't been able to prove he's done anything illegal at all since he got out of prison."

That reminded Jessie.

"Speaking of, I'm going to check back in with Dolan. I texted him on the drive over but haven't heard back yet."

She got out her phone and called. Dolan picked up on the first ring.

"I was about to call you," he said without a greeting. "I just heard back from our overnight surveillance team. They've got nothing."

"What does that mean?" Jessie demanded, putting him on speaker.

"It means they've got cameras in multiple rooms in the townhouse, including his master bedroom and bathroom, living room, and kitchen. He's asleep. He did exactly what he said he would: eat sushi and crash early. He went to bed about ten forty-five. It's not some mannequin under the covers either. My guys say he got up a half hour ago to go to the bathroom, then went straight back to bed. Nothing notable has happened."

"That doesn't strike you as odd?" she pressed.

"What exactly?"

Jessie tried to keep her frustration in check.

"Kyle obviously knows he's being watched. He waves to your agents all the time, right? But today he makes sure to tell them that he'll be home eating sushi and stays visible and boring all night long?"

Dolan sighed. Jessie could hear that he was as frustrated as she was.

"What do you expect him to do, Jessie? He's been as dull as mud since the day he was released. It's the middle of the night. Did you think he'd be throwing some coke-fueled rager?"

"No," she countered. "Those days are probably behind him for now. But he suspects there are cameras in the house. He baits your guys by messing with them sometimes. But tonight it's all by the book. It just seems awfully convenient."

Dolan didn't respond for a few seconds. Jessie knew he was thinking how best to craft a diplomatic answer.

"Jessie," he finally said. "I know your ex is a bad guy. You don't have to convince me. I'm the reason he's being surveilled at this moment. And I believe he's after you. I don't even doubt that he might have been responsible somehow for Garland's death and the attack on Ryan. But doesn't it make more sense that he's having one of the cartel people do his dirty work? I mean, my guys just sent me a clip of him rolling over in bed. I don't know how to square that with what you're alleging."

"The cartel thing does make sense," she conceded. "But I know this man. I've known him for over a decade. I slept beside him in bed for most of that time. I know how his mind works. He wouldn't outsource this stuff to someone else. When it comes to hurting me and the people in my life, he *wants* to do the dirty work. That's the whole point of it."

After what felt like an eternity, in which everyone in the room and on the phone was silent, Dolan finally responded.

"I trust you. And if you say he's doing this, I accept that. I don't know how but I won't argue. I can have my guys go over and wake him up, do a search of the place. It'll likely mean his lawyer will be in court tomorrow, claiming harassment. We'll probably have to close up shop on the surveillance early. But I'll do it if you want. Just say the word."

Jessie looked at Ryan and Hannah, both of whom shrugged. She could tell they were torn between the facts Dolan was laying out and their faith in her. Neither doubted her. But they clearly couldn't square her certitude with what they were hearing.

"No," she finally said to Dolan. "I don't want to mess up the surveillance. Maybe he's waiting to make his next move. I guess they should just keep watching him."

"Of course," Dolan assured her. "I'll tell them to update me if they see anything even slightly suspicious. And if you want, I'll call you right after I hear from them. How does that sound?"

"I appreciate it, Jack," she said, using his first name for the first time in weeks. "That sounds reasonable."

"Okay then," he replied, obviously relieved. "I'll do that. But you have to make me a promise too."

"What's that?"

"Get some sleep."

"I'll try," she told him. "Thanks again."

After she hung up, they all agreed to try to get a few hours of shut-eye. Hannah went to her room and Jessie and Ryan to theirs. At his urging, she consented to take one pain pill, as much to make her drowsy as to relieve the discomfort in her back.

"You're going to have to set multiple alarms for tomorrow morning," she told him. "I'm worried I'll sleep right through my normal one."

"Already done," he assured her, smiling. "In addition to your phone and mine, I reset both our bedside alarm clocks. I also texted the overnight desk sergeant and asked him to give me a wakeup call in the morning. So I think we're set."

"My knight in shining armor," she said, batting her eyes and planting a quality kiss on him.

"Just taking care of the people I love," he said, before hastily adding, "You better get ready for bed. That pill is going to kick in fast."

She started toward the bathroom to get cleaned up, then turned around.

"I love you too," she told him.

He smiled broadly before hopping on the bed and pulling up the covers like an eight-year-old giddy to secretly read a comic book he had hidden under the pillow.

"See you soon," he said.

She could already feel the pain medication kicking in within just a few minutes of swallowing it. Her eyes felt heavy as she brushed her teeth and changed for bed.

When she got out of the bathroom, Ryan was already out. His soft, rhythmic breathing worked on her like a metronome. As her head hit the pillow, she wasn't worried that she wouldn't be able to fall asleep. She was afraid of what nightmares awaited her when she did.

CHAPTER THIRTY THREE

Jessie woke up with a start.

She tried to open her eyes, thick with sleep, and found it to be a challenge. Then she remembered why. She'd taken the pain pill, which had knocked her out almost immediately.

So why am I awake?

One of the major reasons she was reluctant to take the pills in the first place was how groggy and unfocused they made her feel. She felt certain that between that and the day she'd had, she'd stay dead to the world until her alarm went off at 7 a.m. But something had awakened her.

She couldn't hear Ryan's quiet breathing so she gently reached a hand across the bed and felt his familiar, warm body beside her. Forcing her eyes open, she glanced over at him and saw that he was lying on his back. His eyes were wide open and he was staring at the ceiling.

Maybe he should have taken a sleeping pill.

"Bad dream?" she whispered to him.

He didn't respond. She leaned over and spoke a little louder.

"Did you see a ghost?"

Still no response. He gave no indication that he'd heard her.

Jessie propped herself up on her elbow and looked down at him. Something was wrong but she couldn't tell what it was. He was breathing, if silently and shallowly. She put her finger to his neck and noted again that he was warm. He had a pulse, though it was faint. But he was unblinking, entirely unresponsive. She shook him aggressively. Nothing.

Her whole body went cold as a surge of panic gripped her. She could feel her mind starting to spin out of control and tried desperately to reel it back in. Though everything in the bedroom was still, it seemed as though the walls were closing in on her.

She ordered herself to stop, to focus. She pushed up onto her knees and looked around the room. Nothing seemed out of place. Still, she reached over to her nightstand to grab her phone. It wasn't there. She opened the drawer where she kept her handgun and found it was gone too.

She turned her attention to Ryan's nightstand and saw that his phone and gun were not resting in the spot where he normally left them. But there was something in their place: a syringe.

She was about to jump out of bed when she had a ridiculous thought. *Am I having a nightmare?*

She reached down and actually pinched the back of her left hand hard. The sting was real. Suddenly alert, she jumped out of bed and flicked the switch on her bedside lamp. Nothing happened. Then she realized the noise machine they used to block out the sounds of downtown L.A. at night was off too. The power was out. She darted around to the bedroom door, about to go check on Hannah, when she stopped.

Someone did this; if not Kyle, then one of his lackeys. He's probably on the other side of this door.

She hurried back across the room and grabbed Ryan's baseball bat from the closet. As she returned to the door, she glanced at her boyfriend, half-expecting him to give her a displeased look at having commandeered his precious bat. But he continued to stare blankly at nothing.

"Don't worry," she whispered in case he could hear her. "I'll be right back."

She yanked open the door and stepped out into the living room, her hands tightly clasped on the grip of the bat, fully aware that she was a sitting duck. The room was mostly dark. The only light came from small slits in the curtain along the far wall, where the bright nighttime city lights managed to dully illuminate portions of the room.

She was just starting to steal across the room to Hannah's door when she heard a jangling sound coming from the couch. Jessie strained to see what it was. Slowly, Hannah stood up. She was holding something in her right hand. It took several seconds of squinting for Jessie to identify what it was: handcuffs.

She opened her mouth to ask what the hell was going on when Hannah beat her to it.

"Don't move," her sister said. "Don't call out for help."

"Hannah, what are you doing?"

"I need you to put these on," Hannah said, ignoring the question.

Her voice was flat and emotionless. Jessie felt her knees buckle. Had it finally happened? Had her fears about her sister's capacity for darkness been realized at last? Was it possible that she had waited until the people caring for her fell asleep, then gone into their bedroom to drug one of them and handcuff the other for god knows what purpose?

Hannah had seemed to be doing so well. Jessie could have sworn they were connecting; that the girl, despite what had happened to her, was learning to embrace being part of a family unit again. Was it all just a charade? Had Bolton Crutchfield, the serial killer who abducted her, really turned her into someone who shared his bloodlust?

"Hannah," Jessie said, making sure her voice betrayed none of her shock and horror, "we can find a way to work this out. You don't need to do this."

Hannah stared back at her in the dark, her expression hidden in shadow. She said nothing.

"Unfortunately, she *does* need to do this."

It wasn't Hannah speaking, but a deeper, male voice, one Jessie recognized instantly. Before she could reply, there was cracking sound and a large, red glow stick dropped to the floor, illuminating the room in a dull, bloody light. A second later, a figure emerged from where he'd been crouching behind the couch.

Despite the terror rising in her chest, Jessie made sure her words came out clear and calm.

"Hi, Kyle," she said.

"Hi, Jessie," he replied. "Don't you love a reunion?"

CHAPTER THIRTY FOUR

He was even bigger than she remembered. He'd always been a physically imposing guy. But he'd clearly been taking advantage of the prison weight room. Underneath the police officer uniform he was wearing, his muscles were bulging. She suspected he'd chosen a too-tight shirt for exactly this moment, in order to either intimidate or impress her.

She studied his outfit, trying to fixate on small details like the name tag that read "Smith" so that she didn't completely succumb to the sense that she was falling into a dark well with no bottom. As she did, something Hannah texted earlier that night, something she'd barely even registered, came back to her.

Cops didn't find anything suspicious. One is staying outside our apartment. Another is downstairs in the lobby with the guards. The other one left.

The other one left. But neither Nettles nor Beatty had mentioned another officer helping out with either the search or security. Kyle must have somehow learned her address and, using the uniform as a ploy, insinuated himself into the condo. Then Nettles and Beatty arrived. When they left, Hannah likely assumed that "Officer Smith" had gone as well.

But he hadn't. Instead, he'd been lying in wait this whole time as a real cop stood right outside. He'd been only feet away from Hannah while she watched TV, waiting for her sister to return. Maybe he'd hidden under Jessie's bed or in her closet or in the storage closet in the living room. Wherever he'd settled, he'd remained there for hours, patiently waiting for everyone to return and fall asleep. Then he made his move.

"Were you in my closet the whole time?" she asked as casually as she could.

"Under your bed," he admitted. "I didn't know your bedtime routine these days and couldn't risk you hanging up a shirt or something. I can't tell you how disappointed I was when I didn't get to be up close and personal for a little hanky-panky. I thought for sure there'd be some after the exchange of I-love-yous. But I guess you guys were just too wiped out, what with investigating those beach murders, including your senior citizen buddy and your boyfriend's near-death experience this afternoon."

"You've been busy, Kyle," she noted dryly, deciding to fake a lack of fear in the hopes that her body would follow suit. "What did you inject Ryan with?"

"I'm so glad you asked," he admitted, oddly exuberant at the chance to reveal the particulars. "It's a specially formulated paralytic, originally designed by an eastern bloc security service back in the 1980s in order to stimulate ... cooperation with people in their care. Later it was adopted by other unscrupulous organizations ..."

"Like say, drug cartels?" Jessie volunteered.

"Now you're getting it," he replied. "Through trial and error, they've managed to formulate it so that they can give the perfect dosage."

"The prefect dosage for what?" Hannah asked, somehow managing to sound petulant, even under these circumstances. Kyle seemed oblivious to her tone.

"For keeping him from moving while still allowing his lungs to function just enough so that he can breathe. It's a delicate balance. Not enough and he can move around. Too much and his lungs shut down completely. The beautiful part is that he's aware of everything. He can hear and see and feel pain. He just can't do anything about it."

"Sounds like the kind of thing you'd be into," Jessie muttered.

He looked at her with unblinking eyes for several seconds before replying. His stare was icy and she felt like a gust of frozen wind had passed through her.

"Don't be snide, sweetie. You're in no position," he said darkly before regaining his chipper tone. "Anyway, it normally wears off in a few hours, not that he'll be around to feel it. That reminds me, your little sister here is going to put those handcuffs on you. So throw the bat over here. Please don't try anything or I'll have to shoot her with your gun."

He produced the weapon to show he meant business. Hannah looked helplessly at Jessie, who tossed the bat in his direction.

"It's okay," she told her sister gently. "Go ahead and do it."

Hannah walked over. Jessie held out her hands in front of her, smiling at her sister as if she had this under control. Hannah returned the smile, though she didn't look as reassured as Jessie might have hoped.

"Cuff her behind the back, please," Kyle instructed sharply.

Jessie turned around. As Hannah leaned in to attach the cuffs, Jessie bent back slightly and whispered.

"Be ready when the moment comes."

When the cuffs were attached, she turned around and glanced at her sister, who gave an almost imperceptible nod. Jessie, who was being watched closely, didn't react.

"What's next?" she asked as if they were all on a tourist trip and Kyle was their guide for the day.

"Oh yes," he said, sounding almost overwhelmed with excitement. "Big plans, happy to share them. First things first though. Jessie, I need you to sit down in that chair. Hannah, please grab a bunch of plates from the kitchen for me, like a dozen. All china, no plastic, please."

While Hannah did as instructed, Kyle stared at Jessie. She wasn't sure if his expression was one of longing or hatred. She imagined they were much the same for him these days. He sat down on the couch while they waited and leaned in, speaking to her like they were co-workers trading gossip in the break room.

"You're not the only one who studies serial killers, Jessie," he said. "I was watching this documentary on the Golden State Killer. You know what he did? Of course you do. But I'm thinking of one specific detail."

Jessie was overcome with dread. She looked over at Hannah, collecting an armload of dishes, and knew exactly what he was referencing. The Golden State Killer was a serial rapist and killer in the 1970s and '80s in California. One of his hallmarks was to tie up a husband, make him lie face down, and put china on his back. Before he went to rape the man's wife, he warned that if he heard any of the plates fall, he would kill her.

"Who are you tying up?' she asked once she was sure her voice wouldn't break, refusing to give him the satisfaction of a direct answer.

He smiled, clearly tickled that she understood.

"I have my own variation on the theme," he promised.

When Hannah returned, he instructed her to place half a dozen plates on Jessie's lap. Then he had her put the others on the couch and lie down on her stomach. When she was settled, he placed the remaining plates on her, from her neck down to the small of her back.

"Be right back," he said. "Don't go anywhere."

He walked into Jessie's bedroom, leaving her to ponder what moves she might have. She'd told Hannah to be ready when the moment came. But that was more to keep the girl calm. She had no plan for any upcoming "moment."

Her thoughts were interrupted by a loud thud. The cause became clear a few seconds later when Kyle came out, dragging Ryan by the feet. He dropped him next to where Jessie sat and returned to the couch. Looking down at her boyfriend, Jessie stifled a gag as bile rose in her throat. She could taste her own fear.

"So," he said, as if resuming a pleasant conversation they'd be having. "You're probably wondering how this is going to go down. I'm happy to share. It's currently two seventeen a.m. That might make it seem like we have all night together, but we don't. Detective Hernandez here is expecting that wakeup call from the desk sergeant at seven a.m. I suspect that multiple unreturned calls would result in one of your cop buddies downstairs being sent up here pretty fast. And who knows if one of them might come up on his own before then, just to be extra helpful. Time is our enemy, or at least mine, so we're going to have to move fast."

"Just like I remember," Jessie muttered under her breath.

"What was that?" Kyle demanded sharply.

"Oh, I was just saying that you're behaving just like I always remembered," she said, directing her attention to Hannah. "It looks like prison didn't change him that much. He was always so pleased with himself when he came up with a plan and he simply *had* to share every detail, whether you cared or not."

She heard Kyle inhale deeply and knew he was struggling to maintain control. But she also knew he wouldn't take his next step until he was back in his happy, calculating place. He wanted this to go perfectly. And that meant staying cool. His efforts to regain that cool meant a temporary delay in enacting whatever his plan was. And every delay meant more time for her to find a way out of this. That is, unless he lost it completely and just shot them all.

"How well you know me, my love," he said, seething under the charming surface. "Just like how you knew me so well when I was killing people and framing you for it, all the while sharing your bed, even knocking you up."

The memory of just how easily Kyle had played her, how much he'd hurt her during that time, came back in a rush, threatening to overwhelm her. For two years now, she'd blocked out how her own husband had poisoned her, leading to a miscarriage.

Stay focused. Don't let him manipulate you.

"Not so quippy now, are we?" he said viciously, before the veneer of coolness returned again.

Hannah shifted on the ground and one of the plates slipped off her mid-back, clanging loudly but not breaking as it hit the hardwood floor.

"Tricky, isn't it?" he said to her before returning his attention to Jessie. "Here's how it's going to go, no matter how much you try to stall by getting me worked up. There's going to be a horrific scene when folks arrive here tomorrow and it will all be your doing, dearest Jessie."

"Pray tell," she taunted. "What's the genius plan it only took two years behind bars to come up with?"

Kyle's face contorted and before he could stop himself, the words came out through desperately gritted teeth.

"Shut the hell up or I'll cut to the chase and slit the girl's throat right in front of you," he hissed. "You're ruining it!"

"I'm sorry," she said quickly, realizing her ex-husband wasn't as unruffled as he seemed. She couldn't push too hard.

"Thank you," he said politely before continuing. "You've had a rough stretch of late. You smack-talked your superiors in the department and went on a racist screed on Facebook. You were investigated for abusing your own sibling, who was entrusted to your care. You're dependent on heavy pain medication for nasty burns. Your mentor was murdered, a crime you couldn't solve. And to top it all off, your ex-husband, who allegedly tried to kill you, was released from prison, sending you into a tailspin of paranoia."

Jessie didn't mention that the first two items on his list were his doing and that she'd been exonerated on both counts, even if the public hadn't fully accepted that. Nor did she note that neither of the next two allegations was accurate. She rarely took the pills and Garland's killer was sitting in front of her now. Only the last claim had the ring of truth to it.

Kyle smiled cruelly, knowing he'd drawn blood. He happily continued.

"One could understand how that cascading series of events could send you into a deep depression, one you might not be able to pull out of. Friends and colleagues, looking back, would probably wish they'd seen the signs that fateful night, when you returned home, beaten down, in pain, and mourning. You decided it was just too much to bear. They'd be devastated but perhaps not surprised to learn that you killed your own sister and boyfriend, before trying to end your own, now-meaningless life. The note would explain it all."

Jessie took it all in. It was quite a clever plan, almost poetic in a way. If he could pull it off, it would be quite a coup. He would actually be successfully enacting the scheme he'd plotted once before, when he killed his mistress and tried to pin it on Jessie. Two years later, he'd have completed an even more elaborate version, with her going to jail for not one murder, but two. And not for killing a stranger but instead the two people closest to her.

"That's pretty good," she conceded, replying not out of any genuine admiration but because if she didn't speak, she feared she might scream. "But I was confused by one thing. You said I 'try' to end my own life? Do I not succeed?"

"That's still TBD," he admitted. "I'm thinking that after I kill Hannah and Ryan, I'll 'help' you take your remaining pain pills. There are a lot of them left. After the one you took tonight, there are still seventeen. I'm no doctor but I'd imagine that could kill you. Or maybe result in permanent brain damage, or not. It doesn't really matter that much."

"It doesn't?" Jessie repeated, legitimately surprised.

"Nope," he said, pleased that he seemed to have stumped her. "Even if you survive and you still have your faculties, what are you going to do, blame it all on me?"

"I would think so."

"Good luck. Hannah here will have been shot with your gun. I'm thinking I'll take Ryan out with a knife from your set. The note will reference your paranoid suspicion that your boyfriend and half-sister were having a secret affair. It will serve as a confession from a woman who never expected to live. Even if you do survive, your protestations that your ex-husband somehow secretly snuck into your highly secure condo, despite police protection, and managed to kill your loved ones *and* frame you for their murders is unlikely to gain much traction."

"You sure about that?" Jessie countered. "I know some folks in the FBI who might take my view of things." But even before she finished saying it, her heart sank at the answer she knew was forthcoming.

"That's the beauty of it. I'm fully aware of the operation your friend Agent Dolan has going, at least through the end of this week. In fact, I counted on it. He might believe your claims of innocence and accusations of my guilt. But that will only make it all the more painful for him when he has to admit that he has the very evidence that disproves your allegation. He'll have to show the video of 'me' asleep in bed thirty-three miles away at the exact time these murders were committed. It's delicious, don't you think? What better alibi witnesses could I have than the FBI?"

Chapter Thirty Five

The panic Jessie had been battling since this began reasserted itself.

Kyle was right. If this went as he planned, it would be like a boulder pushed down a hill. Unless you stopped it before it started down, there was no way to slow its momentum until it got to its ultimate destination.

If she didn't come up with a way out of this now, then in addition to Garland, Hannah and Ryan would be dead, she would be in prison, and Kyle would be free to inflict whatever sociopathic harm on the world he chose.

Then I guess I don't have a choice. I'll just have to blow up the boulder before it gets started.

"Kyle, while I'm obviously appalled, I have to admit that your plan is pretty ironclad," she said, making every effort to keep any hint of insincerity from creeping into her tone. "But I'm a little confused by one part of it."

"What might that be?" he asked, relishing her apparent puzzlement.

"I have it on pretty good authority that you want to, what was the phrase you mentioned to a fellow inmate, 'gut me like a pig and bathe in my warm blood.' In fact, when I visited you in prison that one time, I distinctly recall you made me a promise. Do you remember it?"

"Refresh me."

"Sure. After all, I committed it to memory. You said 'I'm going to get a tire iron and beat you until you're a pulpy mess of shattered bones, shredded skin, and oozing blood. It's gonna be special.' Does that sound familiar?"

Kyle stared at her coldly.

"What's your point?"

"Well, if I'm locked up for a double murder, you won't get to deliver on that promise. Even if I get the death penalty, it won't be carried out for a long time and it won't be you doing the deed. I just thought you wanted to be more 'hands on.'"

She watched as he looked away, turning over the notion in his mind. As he did, she glanced around for anything she might be able to use as a weapon. Of course, even if she found something, she didn't know how she'd access it with her hands cuffed behind her back. When she saw him look back at her, she made sure her expression was one of true mystification, devoid of disrespect.

"It's not as big an issue as you might think," he told her. "In fact, now that I think about it, there's something extra satisfying about the anticipation. If you ever do get out, which we both know is doubtful, I'll be waiting for you. And if I ever get tired of waiting, rest assured, I'll be able to get to you. I have resources at my disposal. In the meantime, while you rot, I'll be out enjoying the fruits of my new association."

"I assume you're referring to the Monzon cartel in Monterrey?"

"They're very generous to those who exhibit loyalty," he confirmed, grinning.

"They'll eventually learn what we all do when it comes to you, Kyle."

"What's that?" he asked.

"That you're not as loyal as they might think and that, in the end, you're not worth their trouble. When that day comes, it's going to get ugly for you."

"Maybe," he acknowledged, not as offended by the charge as she would have expected. "But in the interim, I'll have a great time on their dime. Maybe I'll engage in some risky, potentially criminal sexual behavior. I'll send you postcards so that when you hear about the victims on the news, you'll know who did it and that you're powerless to stop it in the future."

"That's your fatal flaw," she said, sensing that the time for talk was fast concluding.

"What is?"

"Always assuming I'm powerless. I'd think you'd have learned your lesson by now."

He didn't respond to that, instead shoving her gun in his waistband and moving over to the kitchen. Jessie knew immediately what he was after: one of the knives from the knife block sitting on the breakfast bar. And in that moment, she realized that for this brief period she had an advantage.

Kyle couldn't kill her, at least not with a knife or gun. If his scenario— Jessie kills her loved ones and then attempts to commit suicide—was to appear credible, she couldn't be found with gunshot or stab wounds. He had to show some restraint.

This was her window, when neither Hannah nor Ryan was in immediate danger and Kyle was vulnerable. So she took it. Jumping up and ignoring the plates that fell from her lap and shattered on the floor, she ran toward him. He turned around just in time to see her launch herself at him.

The collision was forceful. Jessie made direct contact with Kyle's chest area before tumbling past him and slamming her shoulder hard into the side of the breakfast bar and sliding to the floor. Multiple screams of pain rang out in the dimly lit living room.

It took a second for Jessie to realize that one of the voices was hers. Her left shoulder was throbbing in agony and she immediately knew that it was dislocated. She looked over to see that, though he was still standing, Kyle was doubled over, clutching his right clavicle with his left hand. A half cry, half moan was emanating from deep inside him.

Jessie shut out the pain and tried to scramble to her feet. But Kyle, glancing at her through watery eyes, saw what she was doing and kicked her down again. Her back slammed into the base of the breakfast bar. For a brief moment, the pain in her shoulder was masked by the stinging sensation in her back.

"That was a mistake," Kyle grunted as he stood upright and turned back to the kitchen counter.

Though she couldn't see it, she knew what he was doing. The sound of a blade being unsheathed echoed through the room. A second later, he bent down to show her the chef's knife. She took no solace in the knowledge that it hadn't been sharpened in years. It would still do whatever job he had in mind.

He stepped away from her in the direction of Ryan and Hannah, who was getting to her knees, sending a new round of plates shattering to the ground. As he moved away, Jessie kicked out her leg, tripping him.

He sprawled to the ground, landing hard. She heard him howl in pain a second time and realized that something was clearly wrong with his collarbone. In fact, as he got to his knees, he switched the knife from his right to his left hand.

In that moment Jessie flashed back to the morgue where the coroner had described the hematoma on the back Garland's skull. Suddenly she knew exactly how he'd gotten it. When he threw himself back into his assailant, he hadn't made contact with his face. But he had connected with the man's collarbone. Apparently he'd done some serious damage. And more than that, he'd left one final clue as to the identity of his killer.

Despite his obvious physical distress, Kyle glanced back over his shoulder at her with a triumphant grimace on his face, and then turned back around. Without a word, he plunged the knife into Ryan's chest.

Hannah screamed. Jessie was too stunned to make a sound. She could only stare at the man she loved, unmoving, likely shrieking in silent agony at the blade embedded in the right side of his torso. Something inside her cracked and numbness washed over her body.

Kyle slowly got to his feet, then pulled her gun out of his waistband. He took several deep breaths before turning to face Jessie. She waited for him to shoot her. She almost hoped he would. Then this nightmare would finally be over.

But not for Hannah.

Somewhere in her desensitized remains, something stirred. Her death would leave her sister alone to face whatever evil Kyle still intended to wreak. And knowing Kyle, that was a lot of evil.

"What were you saying about powerlessness?" he snarled at her. "Looks like you're going to have to rethink that one, darling."

He turned back around to look at Hannah, who was still on her knees, surrounded by a sea of splintered china. Jessie knew what he had in store for her and resolved that no matter how futile, she would try to stop him. She wriggled to an upright seated position and noticed something in between the spasms of anguish emanating from her shoulder.

Now that the shoulder was out of its socket she had a sickeningly wider range of motion. She thought that if she could extend her arm further down, she might be able to slide her butt through the hoop of her cuffed hands and then loop her arms over her feet, moving them to the front of her body.

She waited until Kyle fixed his gaze on Hannah and began talking to her directly, as she knew he would. Then she began the maneuver, biting her lip to keep from letting any cry of pain escape.

"Hannah," Kyle said in a mournful tone, "I'm truly sorry that you got caught up in this. It's not your fault that you're related to that messed-up bitch."

"I'm glad to be related to her," Hannah spat back at him. "She's my sister and I'm proud of her. You're the little bitch."

Kyle laughed fleetingly before the pain in his collarbone made him stop.

"Now I see the family resemblance. Despite your nasty words, I want you to know that I'm not a monster. Okay, I am. But I'm not a *complete* monster. That's why I'm going to make this quick for you. No knife to the chest, just a shot to the back of the head. You won't see it coming. That's my gift to you."

Jessie had now managed her complicated maneuver. Her cuffed hands rested in her lap as she tried to decide how best to make her next move. She saw Hannah glance at her for a split second before turning her full attention to Kyle.

"I don't need your gift," the girl shouted at him in what was an obvious attempt to keep his focus only on her. "You're just a coward who can't look a teenage girl in the eyes while you murder her. I'm amazed you lasted two years in prison. I can just imagine the favors you had to do to survive."

Jessie was on her feet right around the time Kyle responded.

"Last chance to turn around," he growled at her sister.

Jessie was almost to him when he heard her footsteps. He spun around, aiming the gun in her direction just as she swung her arms over his neck. She heard the gun go off but didn't feel any new source of pain, unaware that Hannah had flung her arm out, knocking Kyle's elbow and making his shot fire errantly into a wall.

Jessie used her momentum to slam into Kyle. They toppled over, with her on top of him, and landed hard. As they hit the floor, she propelled her forearms into his chest, hoping to make solid contact with his clearly damaged clavicle.

The collision made them both bounce. Kyle hollered, indicating that she'd been successful in targeting his collarbone. She disregarded her own pounding shoulder as she clambered to her knees to get a better angle to twist the handcuffs around Kyle's neck.

She saw him lift the gun, still in his left hand, in the direction of her head. But before he got it all the way up, two hands, Hannah's, clasped his wrists. For several long seconds, the two of them engaged in a terrifying arm wrestling competition, as the teenage girl used her entire body weight to try to push Kyle's arm down while he attempted to lift it, his vein-choked arm muscles bulging at the effort. Jessie flashed back to earlier that same evening, when another brave young woman desperately used all her strength to prevent a much larger man from hurting her.

Finally, he changed tactics, dropping his arm as he flailed about. As he did, the gun popped out of his sweaty hand and disappeared under the couch. He managed to roll over onto his front and knock Hannah away with one broad shoulder, sending her flying into the couch.

Jessie was now on top of him, squeezing the metal cuffs into his windpipe as she stared at the back of his head. She was just feeling him start to weaken when he threw his entire body up and backward, slamming down on top of her, leaving both of them splayed out on their backs, looking up at the ceiling.

Jessie felt his weight digging into her, trying to squash her into the floor. From her vantage point, she could see Ryan to her right, the knife protruding from his unmoving chest. To the left was Hannah, crumpled in a heap by the couch, dazed but frantically, valiantly trying to get her bearings. Jessie had a momentary flash of Garland Moses, struggling much as she was now, desperately try to escape the merciless crush of a man she'd once somehow loved.

The thought of it all produced an uncontainable fireball of fury in her gut. Setting aside all the pain in her shoulder and her back and her heart, she yanked down on the handcuffs, squeezing the metal chain in the flesh of his neck, picturing it cutting through to the bone of his windpipe below.

She felt him trying to push off the floor with his hands and ripped him back down, using every ounce of strength she had, imagining actually smashing her elbows through the wood of the floorboards.

She heard him gagging, felt his resolve weakening. But just when she thought he'd begun to give up, he flung himself upward again. Her grip loosened and she knew that he was about to break free.

But then, out of the corner of her eye, a figure flew toward them, smashing into Kyle's chest and sending everyone collapsing back to the floor. With Hannah now on top of him and Jessie underneath, Kyle was pinned.

Jessie took a huge gulp of air and redoubled her efforts, pulling down with a reservoir of determination she didn't know she was capable of. The chain of the cuffs cut into the soft skin of her fingers, making them raw with pain. Something she couldn't identify was dripping off Kyle's body onto her face. It was salty but she didn't know if it was blood or sweat.

Despite her best efforts, she could sense that her strength was fading. Kyle's neck muscles strained against the chain like the Incredible Hulk tearing through his own clothes. Still, she refused to let go. Jessie ignored the protests of her body as she clutched the chain tight and pulled, imagining his muscles were ropes that would eventually snap.

He paused for a half-second, before unexpectedly flinging himself upward.

She heard something crack but kept tugging, always tugging, now feeling herself get stronger with each passing second. She visualized herself actually decapitating him and closed her eyes tight as she tried to make it a reality.

At some point—she wasn't sure when—she sensed that Kyle was no longer struggling against her. She opened her eyes to find her sister staring remorselessly at his face. Hannah sensed Jessie's eyes on her and glanced down.

"You can stop pulling," she said with remarkable calm. "He's dead."

Jessie was having trouble breathing.

It wasn't her injuries or the state of shock she could sense was lurking in the nearby shadows of her mind. Rather it was her constant efforts at CPR on Ryan.

At her instruction, Hannah had already called down to Officer Nettles to alert him. She said it was quicker than trying to reach 911. While she was calling, Jessie had evaluated the spot where Ryan had been stabbed, on the right mid torso just above the diaphragm, and made the command decision to remove the knife.

Based on her admittedly rudimentary medical knowledge, she was reasonably certain that it hadn't entered near any major arteries. But it had likely punctured the lung and every time he inhaled and exhaled, even softly, he risked further damage to it. So once Hannah hung up and said EMTs were on their way, Jessie had methodically explained what would happen next.

"I have an extra key to these handcuffs in my bedside drawer," she'd told her. "You get them while I keep pressure on this wound."

After Hannah returned with the key and uncuffed her, she walked her sister through the next steps.

"Get several towels from the linen closet. I'm going to remove the knife."

"Why?" Hannah demanded. "Won't he lose more blood that way?"

"Yes," Jessie told her more calmly than she thought possible. "But the knife is damaging his lungs and his breathing has become shallow and irregular and I'm worried he won't survive until help arrives. I'm going to have to start CPR. I'll need you to use the towels to keep pressure on his wound. There will probably be lots of blood. Don't stop pressing. Got it?"

Hannah nodded.

"But before we do any of that, I need a favor."

"Okay."

"I dislocated my shoulder earlier," she said. "There's no way I can do chest compressions with it like this. I need you to yank it back into the socket."

"Oh god. I think I'm going to pass out."

"You're not going to pass out. You just saw a man die, not for the first time, and you got through that. This is nothing. Besides, I can't do this alone so you're not allowed to pass out."

That was almost five minutes ago. Jessie wouldn't find out until later that Kyle had remotely disabled the elevators before beginning his attack. That meant that Nettles and Beatty had to run up thirteen flights of stairs to get to them. By the time they arrived, Jessie was gasping for air and her arms, already pumped out, felt like strands of spaghetti. Hannah had offered to take over chest compressions but Jessie told her to keep pressure on the wound. She didn't want to tell her that she didn't trust anyone else to do this.

When Nettles and Beatty burst into the room, they didn't ask if they could take over, they just did it. Beatty attached Ryan to an Ambu resuscitation bag while Nettles attended to the knife wound. Jessie slumped down beside them, too exhausted to physically drag herself any farther away. Hannah crawled over beside her sister and wrapped her blood-drenched hands around her.

Even when the EMTs arrived, preparing to take all three of them to the hospital, she wouldn't let go.

CHAPTER THIRTY SIX

"**K**at's here," Hannah said, snapping Jessie out of her reverie. Her friend had pulled up in front of their building and was walking to the lobby.

"Hi, ladies," she said warmly as she looked at their suitcases. "Is this everything?"

It took a second to process the question. That happened a lot lately. Jessie had felt numb for most of the last day and a half.

Katherine Gentry, her best friend, had returned early from her neurological evaluation in Phoenix and had offered to let the two of them stay at her place until they found a new one. Looking at her, Jessie thought Kat's time at the Mayo Clinic, even though it had ended prematurely, had served her well. She appeared rested and in high spirits.

The effects of her multiple concussions obviously couldn't be countered in one half-week stay at the facility. But even in Jessie's anesthetized state, she observed that Kat looked hopeful and healthy. Her dark blonde hair, usually tied up in a bun or ponytail, was loose around her shoulders. Always in good shape, Kat looked like she may have allowed a happy extra pound or two on her normally rock-hard, muscled frame. Even the long scar under her left eye and the pock marks on her face and neck that served as constant reminders of her time in a war zone couldn't diminish her striking confidence.

"It's enough to get us by for the next week or so," Jessie told her. "We'll have movers take care of the rest when I have time to set it up. We just need to be out of the place, you know?"

"Of course," Kat said, not pushing the issue.

"I'll meet you guys in the car," Jessie said. "I just need to turn in the keys at the security desk."

Kat and Hannah went outside. Jessie watched them go for a moment before slowly making her way up the lobby stairs, favoring her aching shoulder. She didn't say it but she was also glad that Kat would be able to help them with everyday tasks they would otherwise struggle with. It turned out that Hannah had cracked a rib when Kyle knocked her into the couch. She was moving gingerly too, trying to take only small inhalations to reduce the ever-present tenderness.

Jessie had fared better than she expected. Some of the burn wounds on her back had opened up again, her hands were bandaged, and her left arm was in a sling. But otherwise, she felt physically all right. How she felt emotionally was another matter.

Despite pleading from both Captain Decker and Hannah, she had refused to go to the funeral. She wanted no part of it. She had buried too many people these last few years. She couldn't do another. When Jack Dolan called and tried to convince her to go, she hung up on him.

She immediately shoved that thought to the back of her mind, so that it wouldn't send her spiraling into the black hole that constantly threatened to consume her. Without the presence of the man she counted on to keep her head above water, the man she'd gotten used to having beside her through each day and night, she found steering clear of that black hole increasingly challenging.

So she chose instead to focus on concrete things that could buoy her spirits. There was *some* good news. Apparently there was an opening at Central Station for a police researcher, so she made sure to put in a good word for Jamil Winslow.

More significantly, within minutes of learning what happened at Jessie's condo that night, Jack Dolan had ordered his overnight agents to raid Kyle's townhouse. They quickly discovered that the man sleeping in his bed was a guy who went by the name of "Rick," and had an impressive fake ID to support it. He bore a striking similarity to Kyle, even close up. They also found a secret tunnel traveling from Kyle's townhouse, under the yard to the back unit of the townhouse one street over, as well as definitive evidence in the home that Jessie's racist Facebook posts had been hacked.

Dolan's bosses wanted to bring Rick in and throw the book at him. But Dolan had other ideas. With their blessing, he made it clear that if

Rick refused to work for them, the Bureau would leak that he was doing so anyway. They would thank him for his assistance in foiling Kyle Voss's plot and sharing the cartel's plans in the U.S. The only way they would *not* leak this falsehood was if it became a fact. Otherwise, Dolan told him, he was essentially a dead man walking.

Facing that possibility, Rick, whose real name was Esteban Huerta, broke. Over the course of a fourteen-hour interrogation session led by Dolan and some colleagues at the DEA, Huerta gave them the particulars on how Kyle managed to secretly escape in order to attack Garland and Ryan. He also revealed the cartel's plan to have Kyle reestablish himself in the finance community and eventually launder their money through the charitable foundation he'd established to help wrongly convicted prisoners.

Huerta agreed to become a double agent of sorts. Once Kyle Voss's death became public, the FBI would come up with a cover story that kept him out of it. When he was recalled to Monterrey, he was to try to rise within the organization, all the while feeding a designated DEA handler with regular information on the cartel. Jessie was glad that there would be at least one positive outcome owing to Kyle's release from prison.

She handed the key to the guard at the security desk, who smiled and nodded but said nothing. She didn't blame him. What could he possibly say?

As she delicately made her way back down the stairs and out of the lobby to the car where Kat and Hannah waited, she reminded herself that there was one other bit of good news. It was related to Barnard Hemsley, the slovenly, coked-up divorce attorney who had made their lives so difficult.

Considering what happened to Ryan later that night, the Manhattan Beach district attorney decided it would look bad to drop charges against a man accused of assaulting a decorated detective, even if that assault amounted to poking a finger in his chest. As a result, Hemsley had an upcoming court date, as a well as a hearing before the California Bar Association. Jessie offered to be a witness at both proceedings.

Kat hit a bump in the road, bringing Jessie back into the present. She looked around and noticed for the first time that Kat had veered off the normal route to her place.

"This isn't the way to your apartment," she said warily.

"Good catch, profiler lady," Kat relied dryly. "We're making a pit stop on the way."

Jessie felt her stomach twist up involuntarily.

"We're not going there," she said emphatically.

"Yes, we are," Kat replied calmly, as if speaking to a stubborn child. "The service starts in twenty minutes. I want to go. Hannah wants to go. You can sit in the car if you want. But we're going."

The remainder of the drive took place in silence. When they arrived at Hillside Memorial Park in Culver City, Kat pulled over to the side and spoke to an officer at the gate. He motioned for a colleague to escort them past the endless stream of vehicles to the reserved parking area. Jessie could see a massive crowd walking toward a grave about sixty yards away. They all sat quietly for several seconds before Hannah finally spoke.

"I know they saved seats for us," she said softly. "I'm going to head over."

"See you soon, kiddo," Kat said.

Hannah shut the door and Jessie watched her fall into line with the other mourners, her head down, her shoulders slumped. Jessie noticed that the girl was wearing a lovely, muted, floral dress.

When she put it on this morning, it hadn't registered that it would be appropriate for either settling in at a new home or attending a funeral. Jessie silently chastised herself for missing the clue before chastising herself a second time for being so hard on herself.

"Okay," Kat said firmly. "Let's have it."

"What do you mean?" Jessie asked irritably, still annoyed with her friend and now confused too.

"I know you're upset, Jessie, devastated even. And I know that the idea of being here right now seems like more than you can bear. But we also both know that if you don't go, you'll regret it for the rest of your life. It'll be another way to pile guilt on yourself and god knows, you've already got a mountain's worth of that. So why are you still in this car and not at that gravesite?"

Jessie sat quietly for a long time, unsure how to respond. But if anybody could understand, it was Kat. She'd lost fellow soldiers during her tours, friends she'd never see again, whom she'd watched get blown apart. The acid brew of death and guilt was no stranger to her.

"I feel like I should have been able to stop it," Jessie finally said. "I knew Kyle was a threat. I knew what he was capable of. I should have pushed harder to take him down. I shouldn't have trusted the FBI to watch him. Nobody knew Kyle like me. Even the people who believed he had ill intent didn't comprehend how clever he was, the depth of his hatred. I should have made them understand."

"You tried," Kat insisted.

"Not hard enough. Or else we wouldn't be here."

Kat sighed. After a few seconds, she tried a different tack.

"At least he's no longer a threat to anyone else. That's because of you."

Jessie nodded. And then, before she could stop herself, the words were out of her mouth.

"I liked it," she whispered.

"What?"

"When I was choking him and I heard his windpipe snap, I liked it. The feeling was satisfying, almost… thrilling. I've had to kill people before but I never felt like that when I did it. What does that say about me?"

Kat took her hand and squeezed.

"All it says is that he pushed you to that point. He was threatening everything you held dear. Stopping him—*ending* him—was your only option. I don't think you were feeling thrilled in that moment. I think you were feeling relief."

Jessie looked her friend in the eye. She couldn't tell if she was sincere or just trying to make her feel better. Either way, it didn't change how Jessie felt.

"I'm not so sure."

There were easily a thousand people at the funeral. Jessie knew it was being carried on closed-circuit television too, with the feed going directly into monitors at police stations all over the city. Though it was a private event, local news was sure to get the footage one way or another and air it to millions.

She took the seat that had been reserved for her, between Hannah and Captain Decker. She wasn't entirely sure when or how she'd changed her mind about coming but she was here now. Kat stood a little distance away.

The rabbi said a few words, and then recited a few prayers. After that, the deputy director of the FBI, who had flown in from D.C., spoke. Captain Decker got up next and talked for a bit. Jessie didn't hear any of it.

At some point she realized there were no more speakers and that everyone was silent. She looked up. Several eyes were on her. She leaned over to Hannah.

"What's going on?" she whispered.

"The rabbi asked if anyone from the family wanted to speak."

"He doesn't have any family."

"That's not true, Jessie," her sister said.

She was right, of course. For some time now, Jessie had known that Garland Moses viewed her as a surrogate daughter. His wife had died young of cancer, though he'd never mentioned that to her. He never remarried nor had children of his own. But without ever saying it out loud, he'd made it clear in countless unspoken ways that he viewed Jessie Hunt as the child he'd never had.

She found, much to her own surprise, that she had risen to her feet and was walking over to the lectern. And then, without really knowing what words would come out of her mouth, Jessie began to speak.

"I only knew Garland Moses for about two years, although of course I knew *of* him for many before that. I was scared of him at first, intimidated, though he never gave me a reason to be. It was his reputation for hunting down the worst of humanity that made him seem fearsome.

"But once I screwed up the courage to talk to him, to seek out his counsel, to get to know him, I discovered that he wasn't so fearsome after all. He was gentle, which he hid by being quiet. He was kind, which he masked by seeming absent-minded. He was warm, which he veiled in crustiness. He was generous, which he pretended was inadvertent. He never once refused me help when I asked or advice when I needed it.

"Most importantly, when I doubted myself and feared that what I knew to be true might be false, he refused to doubt me. He believed in me when I didn't believe in myself and that allowed me to believe again. He was always there for me. And isn't that what family is supposed to be about? Garland Moses was my family and I will miss him dearly."

EPILOGUE

A machine in the darkened hospital room beeped quietly.
Jessie wasn't certain which one was making the sound. There were so many to choose from, so many tubes connected to Ryan's body.

She sat silently in the uncomfortable chair she'd pulled up next to his bed so that she could hold his hand. She'd been here for hours and would stay for several more. Hannah was at Kat's apartment, enthusiastically plastering posters of singers Jessie had never heard of to her side of the wall in the spare room they'd be sharing for now.

For half a second, Jessie thought Ryan had squeezed her hand, but then the hope faded. She remembered that the doctor had told her he might twitch involuntarily on occasion. But that didn't mean he was regaining consciousness or that he ever would.

His condition was still described as "critical" and had been for two days now. When she'd pressed him, the doctor had admitted that Ryan's chances of survival were "no better than fifty-fifty."

"But he's strong," the doctor had added quickly. "And that means a lot. We'll know more in a few days."

If Ryan did wake up, it would be to another world.

The new world, which she hadn't yet told anyone about, was one in which she intended to resign as a criminal profiler for the LAPD. She'd written the letter to Captain Decker in her head. She just had to put it down on paper now.

She was done with hunting serial killers. She was done with losing friends and family to the monsters she'd let define her life. Her mother had died at the hands of one, as had her adoptive parents. She'd lost her mentor to another killer and almost lost her sister to him too. She might well still lose the man she loved. This life had to end.

She knew she could get a teaching position almost anywhere she wanted. Her thesis advisor had adored her. Her therapist, Dr. Lemmon, a former profiler herself, held influence at every major university in Southern California and would surely use it if Jessie asked.

She recalled Garland Moses's words from what ended up being their last conversation, in the Nickel Diner over coffee, just before she'd sent him off with a sarcastic quip, something she now deeply regretted.

You need to take care yourself. If you won't do it for your own well-being, think of your little sister and that dashing detective you love. Those relationships are inevitably going to suffer if you keep your foot on the pedal all the time. Looking out for you helps you look out for them.

She planned on taking his advice. This change would allow her to lead a more normal life, get home at a decent hour, and actually be there to help Ryan recover, assuming he got the chance. She'd be there to help her little sister through the hell that had been her life this last year. She still didn't know if Hannah had helped her defeat Kyle out of genuine love, obligation, or self-preservation. But she had helped and that was a good sign. Jessie hoped to build on it.

With the decision made, Jessie felt something unexpected: liberation. It was as if she'd been carrying an enormous stone and suddenly decided to simply drop it and walk away. Even more, for the first time in what felt like an eternity, here in the hospital ICU, staring at her unconscious boyfriend, worrying about her troubled sister and mourning her dead mentor, she was filled with optimism about the future.

She managed a wry chuckle. Garland would have appreciated the irony.

Now Available for Pre-Order!

THE PERFECT DISGUISE
(A Jessie Hunt Psychological Suspense Thriller—Book Ten)

"A masterpiece of thriller and mystery. Blake Pierce did a magnificent job developing characters with a psychological side so well described that we feel inside their minds, follow their fears and cheer for their success. Full of twists, this book will keep you awake until the turn of the last page."
—Books and Movie Reviews, Roberto Mattos (re *Once Gone*)

THE PERFECT DISGUISE is book #10 in a new psychological suspense series by bestselling author Blake Pierce, which begins with *The Perfect Wife*, a #1 bestseller (and free download) with over 500 five-star reviews.

When a demanding Hollywood starlet is murdered, Jessie must navigate her way through the murky world of film studios, casting

directors, producers, agents, rival actors and an ecosystem of people who may have wanted her murdered.

After one shocking twist after another, the truth, Jessie finds, may be much more unexpected than anyone thinks.

Can Jessie, still wrestling with her own demons, enter the killer's mind and stop him before he strikes again?

A fast-paced psychological suspense thriller with unforgettable characters and heart-pounding suspense, THE PERFECT DISGUISE is book #10 in a riveting new series that will leave you turning pages late into the night.

Book #11—THE PERFECT SECRET—is now also available!

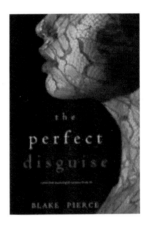

THE PERFECT DISGUISE
(A Jessie Hunt Psychological Suspense Thriller—Book Ten)

Did you know that I've written multiple novels in the mystery genre? If you haven't read all my series, click the image below to download a series starter!

Printed in Great Britain
by Amazon